ALSO BY MOLLY AITKEN

The Island Child

Bright I Burn

Bright I Burn

MOLLY AITKEN

Alfred A. Knopf

NEW YORK
2024

Library of Congress Control Number: 2024937190
ISBN: 978-0-525-65839-9 (hardcover)
ISBN: 978-0-525-65840-5 (ebook)

Jacket illustration by Gill Heeley;
(paper background) Sean Gladwell/Getty Images
Jacket design by Jenny Carrow

Manufactured in the United States of America
First American Edition

For my sisters,
Rosie, Joanna and Alexa

Bright I Burn

Her beard is bloody. She stands on the edge of the forest; beside her lies a dead ram, his neck gaping open. Red in the snow.

My father told me all of Ireland's wildcats were slaughtered by the Romans before those men left our shores, a thousand years ago or more, but once my mother whispered to me, said that when she was still a girl she met a lynx and with her bare lips kissed it.

And here I am, nine winters grown, beyond my city's walls, and my wildcat crouches so close to me I can smell her breath. Flesh and pine. I reach for her, knowing when I grasp her, she will carry me off into the forest and there, with no one watching, we'll dance and whirl and run, run, run.

My hand hovers between her ears. I am ready to be taken, to throw back my head and roar, but a whistle slices between us, and her eyes blaze with fear. Or is it rage? Before I can vanish with her she is become a flash of gold between the tree trunks.

I turn, my eyes stinging with the loss of her, and there, beneath Kilkenny's walls, is a shepherd, his dogs rounding up the flock, and racing towards me across the snow-masked meadow is my mother, her hair flying free from its white cap: the flame of a candle about to blow out.

KYTELER

❧ Whispers ❧

"She's dead."

"Dead?"

"The Kyteler woman."

"On the riverbank."

"At the end of their garden."

"As if asleep."

"Killed, wasn't she?"

"That's what I heard."

"Just the daughter left now."

"The father, a usurer. The daughter, his muse."

❧ January 1279 ❧

A girl comes of age clasped in the jaws of the beast. She must learn to tame it. To stroke its silken fur. To sing it lullabies. To feed it raw meat, and somehow still look beautiful slinking away, whenever it gets too close.

My mother was just fourteen when she married my father. On their wedding day, her purse was empty except for a handful of flame berries plucked from a rowan tree. Her protection against death. She brought with her a rough wooden chest filled with bags of seeds, sprouting bulbs and vials of cures. My grandmother had taught her that the blood moon rising foretells many regrets by sunrise and that a brew of yew needles will slow a heart. None of this my father knew, nor did he care to. She was a woman, his wife. Her purpose was children. Her purpose was me, except she ought to have birthed more than just me, but when I was nine years old I had no brothers and no sisters, and I heard Alma, my mother's servant, tell the cook that the mistress no longer bled. Even then, I knew what that meant. She had lost her value. Even then, I feared for her.

My mother was always quiet. When she did speak, her words described the taste of rain or the shrill call of the blackbird. If I got near her, she smelt of damp green earth, but mostly she was at a distance, digging weeds in the garden or standing beside the deep black waters of the River Nore. It was there, the evening after I met my lynx, that she was strangled.

∅

She is dead seven years now, and not once since then have I met my wildcat again.

These days when I snatch a morning away from the warmth and labour of my father's workroom, I go in search of memories of her or better yet my wildcat, who I sense swallowed some part of my mother on her death and now roams the forest in search of the daughter she has lost.

It's just after sunrise, the sky still pink. I drag my feet through the snow. Sheep scatter ahead, bleating with fright. I ought to hurry before Father sends someone to search for me. Still, I turn back just once to catch a glimpse of a furred head peeking from behind a bush, or the dimples of paw prints in the snow, but all I see are the trees, quiet and cold and distant.

I step onto the slush-churned road. Ahead, the city walls rise grey and damp from the snow, only relieved by the open gate. Kilkenny has nine, which allow for brief escapes by daylight before curfew hits and we must be home, apparently safe in our own beds. There have been no raids by the Gaels, who are after us settlers since before I was born, but no matter. Each night we are locked in.

As I enter Kilkenny I make my back rigid, firm my jaw and fix my gaze straight ahead. Like the city, I must armour myself, not against the blades of enemies, but instead as protection from the whispers of the watchers. I am sixteen years alone in this skin, and with each season, their hunger for me increases.

I pass the castle, obnoxiously bulbous and large, seat of the Marshalls to whom we all must pay our unquestioning gratitude for building Kilkenny up from a mere monastic town to the grand place it is now, flame for the moths: the merchants, knights and all those seeking gold and wool.

This is Kilkenny. Every morning, our guard dog is beaten awake. Every afternoon, I watch the fish seller drag his cart of silver bodies: mackerel two pennies, salmon twelve pennies, a shark your soul.

Standing outside the cloth merchant's guild, my father's friends are wrapped in furs. To avoid their attention, I look up at the roofs which here, unlike most of the city, are too far apart for a cat to jump between. All the merchants pretend gentle godliness, but each of them, in their way, has grasped for my flesh, and I have escaped them all with a smile, a compliment to his clothes, or a vicious remark, depending on what I judge to be his particular frailty. Before they can stop me with their lisping compliments about the colour of my cheeks in the snow, I turn into an alley, where the air is dense with the smell of rotting fish. I hurry down it, stepping into the clearer air of the wider street below. I pass the main door of my family's establishment, Kyteler's Inn. Travellers from all over the world pass through our rooms. Any one of them might be convinced to take me away to live in a land where the air tastes of citrus and raisins, but Father has refused them all. I shake off the impossible and head towards the side entrance, which is accessed by crossing a shitbrook. The garden door appears shut, but I left it unbolted when I slipped out before sunrise. The planks over the ditch have rotted over winter and groan beneath my tread. I glance into the piss runnel, assessing the fall, and see a mass of fur half-covered with snow. I kneel and search for a movement, even slight. There are four, no five, kittens. The mother's eyes are grey, glazed.

"Alice Kyteler." A bright, violent voice shatters the ice air.

The space above me has shifted to make room for something new. Slowly, I stand. A monk wearing a grey woollen tunic lounges in the arch of the wall, the door to the garden hanging open behind him. He has the strange wild look of a sleepwalker, and like all those who inhabit the dreaming, I sense I ought not to startle him.

"You don't look like a killer," he says.

He means the cats.

"Well, you don't know me," I say and stare.

His relaxed stance tells me he knows he's pleasing to look at. I suspect he's three or four years older than I. His skin is uncommonly clear, no pockmarks embedded on his cheeks; nor do any hunger lines frame his mouth. He has the face of a rich man. I know him from somewhere. I just can't yet place him. But I know his type. I have dealt with men who worship at the altars of themselves all my life, and like most of them he wants me to gaze at him with adoration, and so I stare now at the dead cats. Soon, a dog will rip out their eyes and tongues and the bright squishy innards beneath their soft fur.

"I was just speaking with your father about you," the man dressed as a monk says.

Half the unwed men in Ireland have come on their knees to my father, begging for my hand as if I were Heaven and Father the priest who can be bribed for salvation.

"I always knew I was capable of turning a holy man to Satan."

"What vanity," he says. "Your father mentioned you. Not I. You assume I would lower myself to your kind."

We lenders are always hated, but still. I cannot help but glare, and, of course, he laughs.

"As if I would marry into your family," I say. "Oh, yes. I know who you are."

"A man of God."

I point at his shoes which are sewn with delicate embroidery. No monk would ever own such a pair. His smirk broadens, and I hate that I can't seem to pull my gaze away, and this is when the faces of his family appear in my mind's eye.

"Le Poer's your name," I say.

"Caught."

He is John, the son of a baron who is landed in Waterford.

"I don't care which one you are," I say. "A criminal or a baron. You're all the same. Murderers and thieves, the lot of you."

Now, I am smirking.

I expect his face to turn red with fury, but he just rubs his forehead, and suddenly I see the child in him, the boy attempting to convince his father of his quick intellect and strength to hold his title.

"You want to know why I'm dressed as a monk," he says.

"Not really," I say. "Now, move, so I can go into the garden and no longer have to look at you."

He beams. His teeth are uncommonly clean. "Did you never wish to know what it is to be ordinary, unseen?"

"No, and I certainly never will."

I step forward to force him to stride back or sidle around me, but he does neither, and so we're both standing, face to face, inside the narrow doorway. He rests his hand on the wall just above my head. His breath is warm and smells of beer and cloves, and I am almost tempted to take his hand, run now to the church and never return to my father's side. But I don't move. He is the one who reaches inside his tunic and pulls out a small, dark cake. Before I can refuse, he presses it into my hand.

"Bite," he says, and I do.

It's gritty and sweet and cloying. His lips soften into a smile, his mouth almost vulnerable, and I think I could press the tip of my knife against his ribs and he would let me slide it between his bones.

"One day," he says, stepping out of the doorway. "Alice Kyteler."

I cannot help myself. I watch him kneeling on the planks, his hand lost inside the pile of dead fur. I watch him pull out a flame-coloured, mewing kitten. I watch him as he strides towards the river, whistling, one hand holding the kitten against his chest.

🖋

I vomit into the rosemary bush.

My mother's garden is all black and white. At the far end, the dark branches of the rowan tree are dressed in snow. It is pale as a maiden on her wedding day. I try to picture my mother now in Paradise. I see her happy, head turned to the sky, eyes wide and clear and unafraid, but my imagining is extinguished. I was trying to picture a woman who never lived.

I hear someone laugh inside the inn, the clatter of a dropped pewter plate. I wipe my mouth and step through the back door, passing the kitchen without glancing in. A servant in the dining hall is brushing up the dirty rushes. Soon she will replace them with fresh reeds strewn with lavender. Overhead, guests argue in one of the sleeping quarters. We have three. One is large with twelve sleeping pallets. The other two are smaller, each with a big bed, a trundle and a chest. These we keep for the richest travellers, but all guests must have coin, all must arrive on horse, or they will be sent away. By night, I sleep in a tiny attic room with my servant, Old Alma, snoring beside me, and at the door, a boy, armed with a knife, to threaten the drunken guests or anyone else who might stray from their bed.

I stop outside the open workroom door. It is lit by tallow candles and rushlights. The walls are sheathed in tapestries sewn with wolves and bears, and lynxes bleeding. Beneath these hunters' eyes is where I spent all seasons of my childhood. Always taking notes, pushing beads across the counting board, passing a merchant a cup of wine, smiling to ease the sting of the interest on a loan. Always my father was at my side, his eyes sliding over my body, assessing, judging, admiring. Always, I was swift to distract him with a question about solving a calculation, even though I already knew the answer. Next, I would turn his attention to a tendril of useful gossip about a visiting bishop and his mistress. When Mother died, I encouraged him to tutor Roger Outlaw, the son of a banker, three years older than me and almost as clever. His enthusiasm for everything distracted Father and me and brought a lightness to our days. Roger and I studied our trade in the homes and shops of Kilkenny's merchants. A wine seller's wife adopted me for several weeks and taught me Italian. Latin reading, Roger and I gleaned from a lonely monk. All the rest, the note taking, the coin counting, the deal making, we learned from my father. Roger loves my father, and I don't blame him. I do too. Mostly. Joseph Kyteler gets under your skin. His infectious laugh, his ease of manner, his quick compliments, his polished appearance. How could I not love him?

Now, Father is bent over his ledger, humming tunefully. He is seemingly the perfect banker: solid, immovable, all frozen angularity. His jaw is cut with firm lines, his skin white as limestone, and just as powdery, yet beneath the table his feet, nested in fur-lined slippers, tap an incessant, agitated dance. I clear my throat, and he looks up, his face transforming from posed lender into warm, doting father: a common guise.

"Daughter," he says, "you frighten me with this flitting outside the walls. What if a Gael were to grab you?"

I laugh, shake my head. "I'm in more danger between our own four walls."

He rounds his table, approaching me with arms open. He reaches a hand towards my face but stills it before touching my cheek so it hovers, vibrating close to my ear.

"I worry," he says.

I remain still, eyes on the floor, examining every speck of dirt on the chevron planks. I cannot move until he moves, and as is routine with him, he sighs and steps away from me, resting himself with ease against his table.

"I have had another request for you," he says, lacing his fingers behind his head, smug, and I have an urge to shatter his smirk with a biting remark.

"I already know. John le Poer."

"Who told you?" Father snaps his fingers like he does when he loses a deal.

"I have my sources," I say.

"Your sources are my sources." Father smites his thigh. He can be more than patient with a client, but not so with me.

"I just met le Poer," I say, and I cannot quite meet his eye. "In the garden. He was dressed as a monk."

"And what say you to marrying a holy man?" He has softened again. All smiling lips, yellow teeth and smooth brow. His eyes rove my face, and all the while I stare back at him, my gaze steady now we are in conversation.

"Le Poer is the perfect match," I say. "I've always wanted a man whose family is famous for murder and theft."

"Your humour is better served on clients."

"If I was joking, you would laugh."

In two steps he reaches me and takes my hand, which shakes, or perhaps it's his. My mind flits out of me, and I see us as if from above. When I was nine, we danced in this workroom. He grasped my hand, singing a ditty about a baker's daughter, crossed in love between four men. She poisoned each with bread risen in her father's oven. He spun me beneath the arc of his arm, and we pranced across the workroom floor. The door to the hall was agape. I looked up, and there was Mother hovering on the threshold. Her arms were clamped across her chest, and I thought if she let go, she would fall to the floor and shatter.

Now, I am a woman like she was once, and I have flitted out of my body. I see his hand still grasps mine, his thumb against my palm.

"You want your daughter," I say, "living in the house of a killer?"

He drops my hand. I hear him slurp for air. I watch him step away from me, round his table and sit in his chair, head drooping.

"I told le Poer he can't have you or my coin. That's what he wanted. Grasper." He rubs his eyes, his shoulders sagging. "You think I poked a wolf?"

I shake my head. "He's dressed as a wolf but he's a lamb, a murdering lamb."

⌀

It's evening. I sit beneath the rowan tree. Mother and I found the sapling at the forest's edge. It was a wild thing, bent by the wind, ardent to the sky. She took her trowel to the earth, dug it up and instructed a servant to take it home in a handcart. Rowan trees flourish in peace and sunlight, so we had the hole dug at the end of the garden, away from the clatter of the servants and guests, alone at the river's edge. During one hot summer, morning and evening, we dipped a bucket into the water and splashed its branches. We whispered words of encouragement and told it we loved it. In autumn, the berries were radiant, even more bright than those red clusters worn by its mother tree. It was a safe resting place for the tired wings of the dove and crow, a refuge for the cats hiding from toms, a shade for my mother and a lookout for me. To us, secretly and unspoken, the tree was holier than any church.

I look back at the inn, two storeys and an attic, grey walls and shuttered windows. In the stables a horse is kicking. Upstairs a child is crying. An icicle falls from a branch and smashes on the frozen ground. I know he will never let me marry.

It was sunrise when I found my mother. Her red hair was uncovered and trampled into the mud, and on her neck were purple marks, like penny coins left as an offering by the hands of the one who killed her. I wrapped her hair up in my mantle, covering her shame—I would let no one see her hair but me. I curled myself against her, clung on tight. She smelt of river water newly run free from the ice. I don't know how long we lay there, but it was him who lifted me off her, held me at arm's length, examined my hands and touched my cap. My father couldn't meet my eye, and I just knew he had killed her.

❧ At the Fish Seller's Stall ❧

"Old man Kyteler shat himself at church last week."

"Ah, haven't we all. Trout?"

"Not today, thank you kindly. Kyteler's in his bed now, and the daughter's—"

"Running his inn. Not much new there."

"Worse. She's taken up lending."

"She thinks the sun shines out her—"

"I wouldn't say no to her though, if that's what you're meaning."

"Isn't it a shame you're a married man."

"There's ways to wriggle out of marriage."

"Only way I know is through the graveyard."

"That's what I'm saying."

❧ January 1280 ❧

"Your father."

Roger Outlaw is stepping over the garden's plants all bedded down in straw. I turn away from him, straighten my wimple, unclasp and clasp my mantle fastening. I know Roger like I know Kilkenny. I have walked all his paths. Together, we have strolled on the river-bank and crafted a future eating citrus beneath a relentless sun, cooling our feet in a lapis lazuli sea, and all the while my servant Alma watched us, her face wrinkled with irritation because I'd dragged her away from the warmth of the kitchen. Once we stole away from her and raced through the meadow, our hands reaching for each other as we ran, briefly catching hold of each other's tunics, only to lose our grasp as we sped on. We collapsed on the edge of the forest, laughing, sending crows squawking into the sky. I was fourteen, and he was seventeen. I longed for him to climb on top of me and to feel the weight and pressure of him against my body. I waited, listening to him panting, but we both just lay side by side, hands not touching, nothing touching, watching clouds drift until we became too cold and walked slowly back to the city.

Now, on the river a barge slowly glides by.

"Marry me, my lady," the fisherman calls out.

"I am no lady," I shout back. "And I would never marry the likes of you."

Like a mummer in a play, he wails, balls his fists and rubs the corners of his eyes.

"I came as soon as I heard," Roger's voice says from behind me.

The fisherman waves as the barge slides out of sight.

I turn to Roger, try to smile. As a child, his cheeks were freckled, his feet like paws were too large and his eyes, of course, were a deep puppyish brown. Now, his freckles have faded, and he has grown into his feet, but his eyes are still so young, so gentle and mischievous, even now when he's clearly trying to be serious.

"What did you hear?" I say.

"Your father—"

"What about my old man?"

"He is ill," Roger says. "Have you sent for a witch or physician?"

Behind him the inn is grey and bulky. One day it will be mine. One day it will hold more coins than my father ever dreamed of. I gaze back at Roger. One day, even though he has never once admitted wanting it, he will be more influential than his older brother, the lender William Outlaw.

"You're scheming," Roger says.

"I have an offer for you," I say, taking his hand and dragging him to the rowan tree where we are partly hidden from the inn.

He tilts his head to one side. "I'm not sure I want to make a deal with the likes of you, Alice."

He says my name half laughing, half solemn. I feel the tingle of his eyes on my face and step closer to him. He smells of horse and apples.

"I'm the one taking a risk," I say, "going into business with an outlaw."

"My last name is a joke, is it?"

"Of course it is. Now what's your answer."

"What's wrong with your father?"

I silence him with my mouth. His lips taste like almonds. My tongue darts against his teeth. His hands are on my shoulders. Mine are on his neck. We are feathers on a bird's wing, overlapping, but he drags my hands away, drags his mouth from mine.

"What's wrong with you?" I say.

He rubs his bottom lip. His heavy, warm lip. His eyes search my face as if he's looking for the joke.

I can't catch a hold of my breath.

"I'm not set up," he says. "You know I have plans for myself, beyond Kilkenny."

"And you know I have plans for myself too, but I have to marry first."

"You don't have to marry to get rich, Alice."

"*You* don't, but I do."

We stand side by side, facing the river. I think of all the years, sat close, learning to count coins, laughing at the monk who stepped in dogshit, whispering about grasping merchants, waiting to grow up, but I cannot wait for him any more. I look upriver for a barge but find none. My left foot taps an insistent rhythm. I turn and, as I do, feel his hand on mine, but I shake it off, stride down the path towards the inn, march through the open door, slam it behind me, press my back to the wood, hoping to hear him knocking, those lips ready to admit he's made a mistake, but there's no sound of him, and so I turn away, rush down the hallway, enter the workroom where my father no longer sits as ruler.

*

Two weeks ago, Alma gave me a bowl of pottage.

"For your father," she said. "It's your mother's recipe."

After my mother's death, Alma had watched over me. On the rare days I caught a cold she steamed my face with hot sorrel water. When I first bled, she gave me rags to wad against my flow. Always, she watched my father.

"The longer you wait," Alma said, "the harder it will be."

I handed the bowl back to her. "You do it."

She chewed her lip but nodded. "Yes, mistress."

*

My father's bed is monstrous. He is just a tiny head, floating against an enormous pillow. He snores. The flame of the candle flickers and goes out. A cat licks between her legs. On the side table sits a bowl of soup, half eaten. I leave, my mind running ahead of me.

*

William Outlaw's workroom is wide and airy and lit with many lamps. He sits behind his table, head bowed, writing with slow, elegant movements in a ledger. Always, I have known him at a distance, at the Guildhall slowly ascending the steps, at church face pensive in prayer, in my father's workroom voice low and solemn, but his expression softening with fondness when he approached Roger. There are seventeen years between the brothers, and they are as different as a hound from a dove, but despite the distance nothing could break them apart. Except perhaps me.

Now, in his doorway, I am posed in an attitude I know is pleasing. The afternoon light falls over my shoulders, yet he doesn't look up to see the turn of my head, the largeness of my eyes, my muscled arms and legs poorly concealed beneath my tightly girdled blue cyclas.

"What assistance can I offer you?" he asks, his gaze finally fluttering over me.

He remains behind his table, and so I must break my pose and approach him. Today, I wear all my bangles, and they jangle brightly. I dart a look around his floor, trying to note any small gaps in the planks, hinting at a store for money beneath. He seems traditional.

He must keep his wealth beneath his feet, safe but damp and prone to tarnishing. Father keeps our coins behind the panels in the work-room where few would guess to look.

I stop in front of William Outlaw's table.

"I will marry you," I say.

He says nothing, just looks at me, interested yet still distant. He is studied, careful, but this is what I expected from him.

"Your father refused me," he says. "I have already moved on to other candidates."

"Forget these other candidates," I say. "None are as rich nor as young as I, and soon my father will be dead."

"I had not heard he was unwell."

"I would've thought you'd hear it from Kilkenny's whisperers."

"I rarely pay gossip any heed."

"It is often foolish," I say, "yet has its uses."

I turn to the side, rest my index finger in the well at the base of my neck and glance at his ledger, but it is shut. I hadn't noticed him close it. He says nothing, so I let my hand fall from my breast and turn back to face him again.

"I have coin, but I also bring business," I say. "My father's con-tacts are all mine. This year alone, I brought more than half of our deals to signature. I have seen how you work. The women come to you first, and bring their husbands after, but it's the men who come to me."

He smiles, and it is wondrous, disarming and too similar to Roger's.

"My brother judges you to be a likeable woman."

"Does he?"

"He thinks of you as a sister."

"He has said as much to me."

"I will agree to form a union with you." He says this with such formality that if I knew him better I would laugh. Yet his expression is so steady, so serious, I hold myself back. There will be days enough to laugh in future. Years to come together.

"Let's fix a day," I say. "May is always good for a wedding."

"Your father could still be living. It would not be appropriate."

"He has weeks left, perhaps just days."

"I am sorry," he says.

"I am not."

He frowns slightly, but nods, clearly not curious enough to probe me. He stands, dips his hands into a bowl of water, dries them on a folded white linen cloth and walks around the table. Unfortunately, he is a good head taller than me, so I must look up to see his face, pale and delicate and far more beautiful than Roger's. William Outlaw reaches towards me, and, surprised, I take his hand. It is smooth and damp.

*

Father's withered hand reaches from beneath his blanket.

Eight years ago, I watched the servant women comb out my mother's long red hair, wipe down her naked body and clip her fingernails. After she was buried, I collected threads of her hair and her nail cuttings, sealing them in the purse that hangs daily at my waist. I press my hand to it now. When he is dead, I will sell the bed.

"Daughter," he says, "you are so like her."

He laughs, but the laugh turns into a retch. I pass him a cup of water.

In the year after her death, he became gentle, nodding sweetly at the sight of me in his workroom, gazing at the tapestries as if he wanted to step into the wildness of them. Some mornings, I found him down by the river and had to lead him back to the inn, where he nibbled the food I ordered him as if he were a bird. Once I asked if it was our dancing in the workroom, if she had been angry with him, if this was why he killed her. He hit me. After, he sat on the floor and wept. Those were the only tears I saw him shed. I stood over him and watched, waiting for him to tell me, but I waited for nothing. We continued to work side by side, him gazing at me until I felt my clothes were itchy, and I would prod Roger to talk to him or I would leave the room on some pretence, heading for the meadow if I possibly could. But sometimes months would go by, and he wouldn't look at me in that way at all, and I would grow easy in myself, my limbs would relax, and that's when he would rest his hand too long on my elbow, and I would tense. Our dance would begin again.

"Do you think I'll see her?" He smiles, and for an instant, only an instant, I doubt everything.

"You're like me," he says. He laughs until he wheezes until he gasps until his eyes weep from lack of air.

"I doubt you'll see her." I pat his back.

"You think she's already made it out of purgatory."

"No," I say.

His eyes are wide, pretending innocence, but he knows I mean he won't see her in purgatory because eight years ago he took the path that leads to fire.

"You will marry now," he says.

"Naturally."

"You're strong enough alone, Alice."

I wonder if he believes this is true. I try to stop wondering what he is thinking.

"Few would choose a woman banker if she were unwed."

"Possibly," he says. "Well, care for your husband—"

"The way you cared for Mother?"

I can't tell if he's chuckling or choking.

🖋

Out walking in the meadows, I hear the bells of St. Mary's tolling for my new wealth.

I want to break something. Burn a house. Chop a tree. Scream at my neighbours. But I just tuck my wimple into my collar and stride down the Parade, heading home to the inn and my parents' now empty bed.

🌿 In the Graveyard 🌿

"The daughter's guilty, no doubt."

"Guilty?"

"Were you born this morning?"

"She'd never."

"You don't know women, but there'd be no proving it to the court."

"Poor woman, all alone now."

"Poor! Don't I wish I was as poor as her."

"She'll marry soon."

"There'll be a good spread of food at the wedding."

"Not that they'll invite us."

❦ May 1280 ❦

No, Kilkenny has never seen a bride like me. I'm dressed all in scarlet. I have sewn two coins and a hazelnut into my hem, for wealth and luck. The day is bright and cold like the polished silver chain I wear around my neck. The pendant is small, just a sapphire impressed onto a silver square, and on each corner is stuck a pearl. If my husband had asked me, I would have chosen a ruby, to match my wedding tunic, inset in gold, but he will learn my tastes soon enough.

Side by side now, we are an eye-catching pair. Me in my red, him in his deep blue. I have the strong jaw and high cheekbones of one of the stone knights carved on top of St. Canice's tombs, while my husband has the delicate features of one of the saints. He is Theobald of Provins, Giovanni Gualberto. No, no, he is Aurelia, made out of glass and standing frozen in a cathedral window. This heavenly breakable face now looks at me, and I don't smile up at him. I have no need to, and that is a relief. Unlike most of the other men I know, he's never threatened me with his eyes nor his words. He's always been distant, gently kind, and when I was a child, he acted like I was too young to be noticed.

The whole of English Town has come to watch me marry him. The women in clean white wimples, the merchants in their brightest tunics, and the children still damp from washing. Girls, smelling of milk and earth and longing, press meadow flowers into my hands. I drink in their envy, their eyes hungering for my silk cyclas and slippers—my husband. Behind me, men congratulate each other. Money, that's what's on their lips, while the mouths of the girls shape fast to courtly poems, to the wedding night, to the morning after. Blood, I hear them hiss. I smile, pretending ignorance, but I am an innkeeper's daughter; I know just what happens between two bodies at night. The girls' tongues flatten to laugh. I hold my breath, release it in small spurts and give them all my distant, mighty smile. They look away, understanding their place again.

I lead the girls out of the graveyard, steering them by the cleanest route so my wedding slippers are preserved in near spotlessness. The sky feels close and smoky now, twilight falling on us. I hear his name and mine entwined by whispers in tones of awe and fear. *Alice Kyteler. Alice Outlaw.* Together our names spell fortune. Together we spell power.

The girls tell me I look happy, and I tell them I am, and I am. I am richer than I was this morning. I am the envy of the town. I am tied now to a man more beautiful than most, and tonight I shall undress for him and see his eyes widen in fright and pleasure. I shall touch him, press my lips to his, and something I don't yet know will open inside me.

The girls leave me on the threshold of my husband's three-storey house, gasping their "good lucks" and laughing to each other as they prance away.

My husband's street door is well oiled; there's no growl of complaint as he opens it.

He doesn't take my hand, and so I step inside in front of him.

⌀

In my new dining hall, three tables have been pushed end to end. At the centre are four roasted capons, their balls sliced off by the butcher's boy before they'd found their adult cock-a-doodle-doos. I take in the room, noting the average quality of the wall hangings depicting the lumpen men spearing each other. Tomorrow, I will send servants to get mine. The tables are polished to a high sheen. I click my fingers at a servant and instruct him to bring cloths, or if they cannot be got, rushes, to cover the wood. There will be much drinking tonight, many spills. Men's voices in the hall interrupt me. I stand at the end of a table near the door, from where I can easily sweet-talk the merchants and churchmen and watch them cast eyes of jealousy and appreciation at my husband. I arrange my tunic so it falls straighter and look for Roger in the crowd but cannot find him. I didn't see him outside the church either. When the news was announced in town that I was marrying his brother, he left for Dublin, and for days my mind flitted away from Kilkenny, up the coast to him, wondering if our next words would be loaded with loathing for each other's separate futures, wondering if now he would decide to remove himself from Kilkenny for ever in order to forget me.

"Wife," Outlaw says.

"Husband," I say boldly, as if the word is familiar in my mouth.

We watch the men of Kilkenny surge through the door, eager to demolish our food and lick up every last drop of our wine. The churchmen first, always the greediest, dressed in their finest cassocks. Next, the merchants and knights and their assorted wives, all shiftily looking about to see how much coin we spent to impress them. And finally there he is. Roger. Smiling. Yes, he's smiling, and at me. I find my husband is being led away by a priest, and, for a moment, I shut my eyes. When I open them, Roger is in front of me.

"Hello," I say.

"You've married into a family of crooks," he says.

I purse my lips and cross my arms.

"You know," he says, "because of our name. Outlaw."

"I swear I've heard that joke before. I pray you find a better one for your own wedding day."

"I told you, I don't plan to marry for many years."

I want to start over, but it's too late.

"I am sorry," he says.

"For what?"

"For your father. I learned so much from him. I hope one day to be like him."

"No, you don't."

"Tell me what's wrong, Alice." He steps a little closer, but when I step back he doesn't try to close the gap. "You fought with him?"

"I—" I thought Roger had known. I'd thought he'd noticed. I had hoped it was unsaid between us, but it was just me, and Alma, who knew after all.

"You won't kneel to me?" I say.

"What?" His thick eyebrows shoot together, bridging his nose. In the past, he could always keep up with me. Now, he's limping behind.

"It's customary," I say, "when you enter someone's house to kneel, if you are beneath them. What will people think of you slighting your sister-in-law so?"

For a moment, his mouth hangs open. "That's really what you want?" he says.

"It is."

But before either of us can move, him to kneel and I to strut away, William Outlaw is beside me again.

"Your wife," Roger says, "was just trying to convince me to take an action I find repellent."

I feel my neck turn warm, and for the first time today I regret the colour of my clothes.

"She was telling me I ought to marry," Roger says, staring at me, and so I glare back at him and rest my hand on my husband's sleeve.

"My brother is young yet," William says to me. "He puts his life in danger so regularly by travelling that any wife would be severely distressed."

I smile now at William. "You're right. A wife could never handle the tormented freedom of having her husband away from home."

Roger coughs. I don't look at him. I cannot tell if he is disguising a laugh. William's face is unchanged. I can't tell if he is touched or believes I am in jest.

"When you do marry, Roger," William says, "I hope your wife is like mine."

"As near perfect as our Lord's mother?" Roger says.

"You flatter me," I say. "Mother Mary is perfection itself, but I find it irritating that she and virgins like her are the women we always praise. What of the wives? Most women can't remain virgins. How would we continue to people Ireland without women carrying the burden of children?"

Both my husband and his brother are looking studiously away from me.

"I'm not sure faultless women like Mother Mary truly exist," I continue, "but still, Roger, I wish, when you choose a wife, and I don't doubt it will be within a year, that yours will be perfect."

"Let me get you both a cup of wine," Roger says.

With an exaggerated hand gesture and a tight smile, he bows to me and steps away. I have wounded him, but I don't feel elation, only the weight of knowing that on this day I have perhaps forever lost a friend.

❧

The meal is over. Bones litter plates, rice is only half dug out by spoons, and ale is spilled across the lot. The revellers walk my husband and I to the stairs, cheering as we begin to ascend. Before we have reached the top, I turn back to wave at them, but they have all returned to the dining hall to eat and drink without us, all except John le Poer, dressed in a deep purple tunic. I hadn't noticed him enter the throng, nor did I see him outside the church, although I did scan the many men to see if he was among them. Now, he slowly lifts his hand to his mouth, kisses it and blows up to me. Before I can respond, he turns away, into my new dining hall, singing a song too bright and melodious.

*

Candles sputter in the draught, throwing the light about so I can't see the details of my new bedchamber.

I step out of my slippers, shed my scarlet cyclas, leaving a red pile at my feet. My husband bends and folds it, neater than any of my servants have ever done. I step out of my wool inner and stand naked, watching him.

By the half-light, it looks as though his face has turned red. My body has the power to change the colour of his skin.

"Shall I kiss you?" I ask.

He wets his fingers at his lips and walks about the room, the candles hissing out at his touch. In the dark, I lie on the bed and listen to the patter of his feet, the sigh of the bed as he sits on it.

This is the moment. The hands will grasp, the breath will become ragged, insistent. But my hands lie still on my chest and my breath is steady. I am waiting for him to take me in his arms and do what he must. I am terror and also, yes, curiosity, and even excitement. I have seen dull and steady women transformed into wild creatures. They are what I'm waiting to become.

But I wait and wait until the morning comes.

OUTLAW

✢ February 1281 ✢

Kyteler's Inn. How I missed it. So many people come through the doors: the monks, leery and starving for women's flesh—we all know they get enough of each other's; the merchants (wine, leather, cloth, seed and wool, wool, wool), brazenly telling me where they're sleeping, as if I don't know; the servants, two or three to a bed, some housed in the stables if we're full; sometimes the knights (old, young, dying)—Butler, all whiskers; the Marshall cousins red-faced from drinking; a de Lacy with a nervous laugh; and they all deign to come into the workroom of an evening, and I send them all to bed with a loan.

Sometimes, I am tempted by them. Some men smell like pears or cloves or rain. Some sing with heart-shattering voices. Others make me laugh. I am not cold to them, but nor am I a fool. Lying with any would be death, sooner or later, either by disease or by my husband's right to kill me for adultery, although knowing him, he'd hire someone else to do it.

Often John le Poer appears, unexpectedly, beside me. Always, I freeze, unable to say more than a common greeting, and, smirking, he saunters away. Once he is gone, I feel shrunken, and I long to flee, to lock myself in the workroom and touch myself.

The only man with any calming presence is him with the eloquent hands and graceful long neck. Him with the soothing voice, with the knighthood and all his land in Tipperary. Richard de Valle. Whenever he visits, he sweetly thanks me for my hospitality. He is as quiet as my husband, and yet, unlike my husband, I am almost sure, he likes me as a person, because twice while staying at the inn he's stopped to ask, *how are you doing in yourself?* That's how he phrases it, *in yourself*, and on both occasions, I didn't know what to say, and instead turned the question back on him, and as he answered, his large blue eyes seemed worried, not for himself, but for me, and I thought I might cry, so I swiftly dismissed him and walked down to sit a moment beneath the rowan tree.

✑

A servant has lit the brazier on the garden's path. In the street beyond, a horse is whinnying, metal screeches on metal. Someone is readying to leave Kilkenny. Smoke clings and swirls around the rushes, but at its centre the river is black. I am beneath the rowan tree, melding into the darkness. If I were living in a traveller's tale, my mother's tree would now drop down a dress spun from gold, and, wearing it, I would go to my husband and he would finally take me, ripping the fabric, tearing into me like a wolf his supper. But this is not a story. It is my life.

The back door opens. My husband stands just inside it. Since I convinced him to move here he has avoided my mother's garden. I suspect the green disorder disturbs him, but even now, though it's winter and all the plants are hidden beneath the soil, he doesn't step out. Perhaps he senses the shoots of new life readying to explode through the surface and overtake the land. He is waiting, it seems, for someone, but certainly not for me. I am waiting for my life to move forward. He, I sense, is hoping for his life to return to what it was before he married me. I'm sure he's considered how a man might rid himself of a wife, but he's too lethargic to act. He won't even move to enter me at night. If he did, he might get his wish and lose me to birthing a child.

Now, I don't move. I don't want him to see me. I came out here to get away from him, to breathe deep so that I wouldn't snap at him in front of our guests. I have learned by pains it is pointless display-ing my irritation. He doesn't seem to notice the emotions of anyone, especially not mine. For a year now, I have brought in new clients, brokered deals far better than any of our competitors, but as soon as I lead the moneyed men and women through the workroom door my husband dismisses me. He thinks I am like a rose on a party table: beautiful but almost useless.

A barge slides by, and a man leaps onto the bank. He slaps his knees and laughs. It's Roger. He hasn't seen me, hidden by the dark-ness and the rowan's branches. He runs up the path towards the inn, and as he reaches his brother, he talks fast, his hands vigorously giv-ing shape to his words. William's replies are short and low. Already they've shut the back door.

I march up the path, yank the door open and find the brothers standing by the workroom door. William gives me a brief nod.

"Alice." Roger strides down the hallway and falls to his knees. "An appropriate enough greeting for you, sister?"

I can't help but laugh. "It will do."

He leaps up.

"Soon," I say, "you'll be Justiciar of Ireland, I don't doubt it, and you shall have me kneeling to you."

"I wouldn't dare."

There's a warmth in my belly. We are friends again.

"Wife," says William, "Roger and I will be speaking alone. Please ask a servant to bring us wine."

"Men's talk?" I say to Roger, my voice dripping sarcasm.

"Men's talk," he says, echoing my tone.

"I'm sure such talk will inspire a change in my husband's nightly habits."

"What?" Roger says, his voice vibrating irritation. He doesn't want to know what happens, or doesn't happen, between his brother and I.

"Men's talk." I spin around and march back into the garden. There's a whooshing in my ears, and my feet slide from beneath me. I have fallen on the frost-hardened ground. Above, the night sky is horribly vast. It is lit with uncountable fires. My breath plumes above me, obscuring them.

—

❧ The Inn's Kitchen ❧

"He's limp. Limp as a limp fish."

"You'd think ones so pretty as them . . ."

"The more like angels their faces, the more like devils their genitals."

"The master is so very pleasing to look at."

"I've always preferred a man with a less girlish countenance. Give me a rough shepherd. A man that'd strangle a wolf."

"I like men who look like the master."

"Well, if you marry a man like the master, you'll need to charm what hangs between his legs. If the mistress would only come to me, I would tell her how to manage it."

"Tell me, Alma. I'll try him myself."

"Rather you than me, but here's what you do. Get a live fish. I find a lamprey to be a good size, but you may prefer a brown trout. Insert the chosen fish alive inside yourself. Let it wriggle around for your pleasure until dead—quit your laughing. Once dead, take it to the kitchen and cook it in the way your husband likes his fish. The master prefers boiled to fried. Once he's eaten it, he'll be more virile than you could ever imagine."

❧ April 1282 ❧

He is a lump in the bed. Pale hair against the pillow.

I stand above him, squeezing the handle of the lamp, wishing I could hurl it onto the blankets and set him alight.

"What's wrong with you?"

He makes no sounds, no movements. I have heard and seen every type of sleeper, but none so silent as him.

"You." I am shouting. "Do what you're meant to do."

He climbs out of the bed and sits on the edge, facing the wall instead of me.

"Please," he says in that laborious way of his, "put the lamp down. You'll set the place alight waving it about like that."

"Every man who comes through these doors begs for me, but you who lie beside me every night won't touch me."

He says nothing.

"Why do I repulse you?"

"Please lie down." He sounds exceedingly tired. "If that's what you want."

He is still sat on the edge of the bed, staring into the dark, and now the moment is here for me, I don't know what to do.

"Lie down," he says.

I lie out on the bed, my limbs stiff, despite how I will them to be pliant. I know if my body is relaxed, it will hurt less. He leaves all the candles and lamps alight. How I wish he would blow them out. How I wish I didn't have to see. But I see as he climbs clumsily onto the bed, thick wool tunic tight at his neck and reaching to his feet. I don't see how he will manage to get out of it. I have never once seen him naked. Not in almost two years of marriage, but still the moment has somehow come. Finally, it has come, and yet I can't stop thinking of my wedding night, when I was all full up with hope and want and fear. Now, I am only rage.

"I will be quick," he says.

He is not quick. He works on himself to be ready, and when he is, he cannot seem to find my entrance. Finally he manages, and it's excruciating. I want more than anything to bite and scratch him, to shriek, but I force myself to stay quiet and breathe. I stare fixedly over his shoulder at the ceiling. He labours against me so long I feel he has reached so far inside me my mind is about to crack in two. He stops, but I don't believe he expels his seed. He certainly doesn't cry out. He just gets off me and goes straight behind the screen to wash.

I tear off my damp inner tunic, crawl off the bed and rummage in my mother's chest for a replacement, but all my clothes smell of mould. Undressed, I lie under the blankets, shivering, bleeding and not at all relieved. This is what I wanted. This. But it wasn't what he wanted, and that's what's wrong. Two must want to couple. Two must want pleasure. Nothing about him ever wants pleasure. Not even when eating summer berries does his mouth seem to enjoy the taste. I do not have my answer about him. I have no idea why he doesn't want me, and I don't think he knows either. I think he has never wanted anything. Woman, man nor beast. This is what stands between us: his satisfaction in a life lived by the pen and ledger. A monk's life. A life I thought I wanted too.

"Next week," he says from behind the screen, "I shall try again."

🌿 At the Market 🌿

"There's one caught in her belly."

"She's just eating too many cakes."

"I would if I were her."

"I'd drink all the wine in Kilkenny."

"She's with child."

"Doubt it's her husband's."

"My bet is it's the brother's."

"She'd never risk losing her coin, and her life, for a pounding by the brother."

"A good pounding is worth dying for."

❧ May 1283 ❧

It's May Day, and I am hosting a party. As is custom, I have bathed my face in meadow dew. Now, I stand with my aching back against my mother's tree, blossoms floating lazily down around me. Out here, my only company is a flame-furred cat. I click my tongue against my teeth, and she leaps into my arms, her tail swooping around the protrusion of my belly. Since I fell pregnant, even before I myself knew a babe was rooted in me, this creature rubbed against my ankles day and night. Her presence makes William sneeze, and so he has taken to avoiding me, even sleeping on the workroom settle and on some nights returning to his old house. These days, he pats my belly fondly when I pass him in the corridor, telling me he hopes it is a son, as do I because if it is a son, and if he lives, my husband and I need never couple again.

*

Alone, I enter the dining hall. I am dressed in a blue taffeta cyclas loose about my pregnant belly but with sleeves sewn tight to reveal the shape of my arms. Alma will have to cut me out when the party is over. I stride up and down the trestle tables, tasting the dishes, checking the wines.

The guests arrive in clusters, and I insert myself into circles to share a tendril of gossip, dish up advice, pass judgement on choice of dress. I make sure their tumblers are winking with wine or beer and instruct them to taste the roasted almonds. They laugh. They agree, the honey glazed pears *are* divine.

I spy John le Poer, that endless smirk on his lips and his wife on his arm. She has given birth to two children in swift succession, proving he gave her no respite. They approach: her, shy and fumbling; him, as always, comfortable, shoulders sloping down, eyes glancing about the room. His is an air of one who is always at their ease. He and his wife offer up polite words of gratitude for my invitation, but both of them stare too intensely at me, two sets of eyes smouldering for different reasons: hers for envy and his for covetousness. I thank them for their attendance and move swiftly on to a wool trader I have known all my life.

The latest Bishop of Ossory, a red-cheeked man, grasps at a serving girl who shifts away, her expression blank. I give him a tiny nod, but he takes it as an invitation to approach. He leers at my gold necklace as he delivers a chicken leg to his mouth. I focus my gaze just over his shoulder, half listening to some complaint he's making about the lesser le Poers thieving his cattle, make the sign of the cross when he appears to be winding up and tell him I must speak to a dear friend. His shoulders fall. I swing away.

Richard de Valle is alone, as he so often is, watching the crowd with a distant smile, nodding to everyone who passes. I can tell by how they stop and smile, sharing a few words with him, that he is liked by all.

"I am surprised you accepted my invitation," I say.

"I was grateful to be asked."

I prod him about his new wife, and he blushes, points across the room at a small, plain girl with a wide forehead and large blue eyes. I search myself for compliments for her, and he looks so gratified at my deliverance of them that it becomes easy to give him more. I tell him to feed her up and not let her fall pregnant too often. I recommend a witch who is known to make an effective drink to reduce the chance of catching a child inside.

"Thank you," he says. "I am indebted to you."

"Now that you are not," I say. "You are one of the few here who doesn't owe me a single coin."

But he is still caught in previous words. He is gazing at my own enormous belly, fear writ in his tight mouth.

"Don't worry," I say, hearing a small tremor in my voice. "I am very strong, and after this one, if it should live, I won't have many more. I am a woman who takes her own advice."

"I am glad of it," he says, his smile tender, his eyes still holding concern.

I leave him, because if I do not, I will stay all evening at his side.

Roger shows himself, as he so often does, when I have given up hope of laughing. There he is in the midst of the crowd, smiling, and still wearing muddied riding shoes. He waves at me, and I smile back but I don't approach him. Tomorrow we shall pull apart this evening, laugh about the wandering hands of the new bishop and discuss which merchants we should avoid giving our custom.

I approach a group of wives who, from their covert glances, I can tell are talking about me. It is a pleasure to disrupt them and hear them frantically grasping for a new subject.

This is when le Poer's wife appears at my elbow, her skeletal body inserting itself into my presence. She smiles through gritted teeth, clearly preparing to deliver me some sharp, poisoned words, but I touch her shoulder, eyes saying I am no threat, she merely imagines it, and I watch her bottom lip tremble, her eyes widen and search my face as if looking for a doorway to leave by; but if I had one, I would have left myself already. We say nothing, just gaze at each other until Outlaw appears, raising a thin finger at me to signal his arrival, and she, shaking her head as if nothing had passed between us, walks back to her husband. Outlaw's pale hair is oiled, and his deep blue tunic sways about him. We are two water creatures, surely ideally matched in the eyes of everyone now. My belly is the proof of it.

"Wife," he says, "ought you not to rest now?"

"I am fine. Let me enjoy myself."

He bends slightly towards me and says, "You know best."

He walks away, and I am left thinking there is substance in his words for once.

A tall man approaches me. In a single glance I assess him: ugly, teeth too large for his jaw; by a far reach the richest man in the room. His girdle tells me all. It is fastened with a gold buckle more finely soldered than any I have ever seen.

"I hope," he says in French, "your husband has just been complimenting your beauty with tears in his eyes."

"I won't stop you," I reply in the familiar tongue, "if you wish to give him some instruction on the matter."

He throws back his head and laughs.

"Are you sleeping at the castle?" I ask.

"Caught." His accent is English. "I am with my friends." He blindly waves his hand around. "They say you are a woman to know."

"I can tell you're a man who can decide that for yourself."

The harp and flute players have begun a tune, and already people are clearing space for dancing.

"Shall we?" he asks, and I assent, leading him to the top of the dining hall.

I take the first step, and he, smiling, follows my lead but more daintily than me. I clap in admiration, and others join me. He shakes his head, laughing, and passes me across himself to the next partner. There is a dull ache in my back, but I ignore the sensation and dance on. I spin away from my partner, swift despite the great weight of my belly. One last flourish, one last skip down the room, passing through arms clasped aloft in a human arch. Finished, I'm panting. My dance partner takes my elbow, and I allow him to guide me into a chair. I instruct him to fetch me some wine, and, dutiful, he crosses the hall, stopping to talk to everyone, because everyone wants a piece of him, even though they must know he and his coin are now mine. I have discovered he is the man who holds the key to England's coffers, and already I have secured his promise to return to me tomorrow; and once a man is in my workroom, he rarely leaves without a loan.

The heat of so much breath has wilted all my green garlands. I pull myself to standing and step out of the dining hall. Just a few moments beneath the rowan tree are all I need. Just a little cold air to waken me.

"Hello, little cat," says the crisp voice of John le Poer behind me.

I am lifting the latch of the back door.

"You've taken too much of my wine," I say, without turning.

"You don't wish to see me," he says.

I turn. "Well?"

"Well," he says, opening his hands, "you will need a companion outside. It's not safe for a woman alone."

He takes a few steps towards me, but there is still half the length of the hallway between us.

"Out there," I say, "that's my own garden. There's nowhere I'm safer. Return to your little wife, for if you don't, I fear she shall murder me."

"I have not permitted her to buy a knife." He is now just a few steps from me. "You have nothing to fear from her."

"Just because you believe she doesn't own a knife, doesn't mean she's not always armed." I turn away from him, pick up a lantern and step into the black shushing garden. "Don't think about following me," I say over my shoulder. "My strongman is in the kitchen. One call from me and he'll come running. It's dark out here. He might accidentally kill a man he finds disturbing his mistress."

I walk slowly away from the inn without looking back, pleased in the knowing that he watches me, trusting I have frightened him off.

The garden is cold; there are no stars. The only light is the river reflecting orange torches on the water's edge. Soft brown shadows flit towards me. They are moths birthed in the dark and drawn to the light of the lantern. Tiny wings tap my body. I reach my bench beneath the rowan, and my lantern illuminates the outline of a man already sat there.

"Can I not have a moment's peace?" I cry.

"Sorry." The voice is Roger's. "I'll leave you be."

"Don't," I say. "Stay with me. You'll keep the dogs away, and your voice makes me feel lighter. I am so heavy these days. This belly."

"The blessed child," he says. "I'm looking forward to meeting him."

"Are you drunk?"

"Stone-cold sober. Only had a jug."

I laugh. "Well, in that case, I have a complicated business dealing to quiz you about."

He yawns. "Tomorrow, please, or better yet never. What I want to know is how are you?"

"You know me. I am always well."

The river spatters water onto the banks. Roger is now one of them. The order of bankers. My greatest enemies in business. Their reach is beyond Ireland's borders, perhaps into countries I have never heard the name of. They would never accept a woman to join them, and so I must watch Roger at a distance and feel my envy grow. Yet this has always been the way with us. He gets what I want with ease, but his easy character makes me forgive him, almost instantly.

"How are you finding marriage to my brother?" he says. "He is a tough . . . nut."

I have always known if Roger speaks in jest, but tonight I cannot tell. I look up at the sky. Like an ear against a door, the silver curve of the moon presses low in the sky.

"William and I have found our way," I say.

Soaring laughter issues from the inn, and I feel a surge of nausea. It rises into my throat, piles into my mouth and I retch onto the ground. I gasp and retch again. I take in mouthfuls of cold air.

"Have you?" Roger says.

"Have I what?"

"Started."

"What?"

"To labour."

He holds out his hand and I take it.

"I think so."

He squeezes my fingers because there is a chance this is the last night I will see him or anyone. I let go of his hand and open the hatch of the lantern. The moths dart in, and their wings singe, blackening the sides.

How to Check Your Baby Is Alive

Stare into his eyes. Watch the life flicker.

Unwrap him often.

See again that, yes, his limbs are all attached.

Count his fingers. Next his toes.

Hold a feather above his mouth.

Does it flutter? No! Blow up his nose.

Listen to his cries. Shush.

Listen to his silence. Pinch. Then shush.

Again, pry him from the arms of his wet nurse.

Whatever you do, don't you dare sleep.

❧ June 1283 ❦

"Isn't he beautiful?" I say to Roger.

"Will you listen to me?" he says.

I am in the workroom. The wet nurse sits on the settle feeding the baby again. Her arms are so large I can barely make him out. I cross the room and kneel on the floor beside her.

"Alice, you must sleep."

"Leave me be."

"Listen, for once."

I rest my hand on my baby's soft skull.

"If you don't sleep, you won't be yourself any longer. You may forget to collect interest on a loan."

"I would never."

"I have arranged a retreat for you."

"I'm not leaving him. I'm his mother."

The wet nurse snorts, coughs, shushes my baby, stands and strides out of the room. I long to rush after her, but I hold my breath, count to ten and stop myself. I turn back to Roger.

"Don't you fear ending up like your mother?" he says.

"I . . . Why would you mention her?"

"I'm sorry. I'm desperate. May I take your hand?"

"No."

"It's been five days. Have you been outside?"

The brazier spits flaming sparks.

"Look," he says, "if you don't sleep, you're a danger to baby Will."

I watch a spark skip across the floor, land on the corner of my green tunic and burn a small black hole.

"I will go, but for a week. No more."

*

When I arrive at the convent, the sun is a lurid orb. I wait at the small door in the high wall for a nun to answer my knock. The sky changes from grey to blue to grey again. The door leaps open, and behind it stands a young woman, her face surrounded by a white hood. She steps through the archway, slamming the door behind her.

"You may go," she says to my servants who have just unloaded my chest.

She waits in silence as they leave my belongings at her feet, remount the cart and trundle down the road. They are my last chance to leave today, and I have let them go.

I turn back to the nun, who is holding up her hand as a gesture to indicate I am not to dare interrupt her.

"There are six of us who live alone here," she says. "We rarely let in those from outside. We wish to maintain an undisturbed contemplation, but we made an exception for you because your husband knows our priest and our priest is persuadable."

"It wasn't my choice either," I say.

She nods, curt, but I am not yet forgiven.

She opens the door again, and behind her is a garden with more flowers than I have ever seen. Beans leap up poles, herbs spray paths, and apple and pear trees stand along the walls. The air is heavy and edible. Behind this spray of colour, the convent is a squat building, roofed in stone tiles and fronted by a colonnade where honeysuckle climbs as if the garden is attempting to sneak into the women's sleeping quarters.

⌐

The first night in my tiny cell, I stare at the blank walls, wishing I could still see the garden. I feel the sun go down inside me. I am all in shadow here, and I shrink with the strange grotesqueness of the silence. I have left my baby. He will forget the feel of my skin. He will forget the smell of my perfume, but I mustn't think these treacherous thoughts. He cannot forget me. I am his mother. I will return to him—stronger.

Still, all night I'm kept awake by phantom cries.

⌐

By day, I pace the garden, my mind jittering. I pore over my ledger but soon find there is little to assess. Each deal was the best I could make it given the circumstances I found myself in, and there's no changing it now anyway. I have received a brief note from my husband stating our son is fat and healthy. I weep on reading it and keep it against my skin all day and night. Never shall I cherish William's words more than now.

The days begin with songs seeping beneath the door of my cell. I join the nuns and sing with them, my voice shaking at first, but growing in strength, and even some beauty, with each new hymn. For long moments, the chapel wavers in my eyes and vanishes, and I am in my mother's garden, holding my son's hand. He is grown, nearly a man, past the dangers of babyhood and boyhood, and has burst muscled and joyful into manhood. Each day, I sing, and each day, this is what I reach for, my baby, no longer a baby, but a man, safe.

∅

I am strolling along a narrow path bordered by violets, poppies and foxgloves. Food for the bees who hum all about, ready to sting should I disturb them from their labour. My nun finds me bent, watching a butterfly drink a droplet from the petal of a rose.

"Come," she says.

I follow her to a small, dark room with shelves climbing up to the ceiling. Each one is piled with more manuscripts than I have ever seen.

She laughs at my expression. "I saw you reading your little book."

"My ledger. I'm a banker."

She doesn't ask me about myself. She's not interested in my life beyond her walls. She's too content here, or perhaps just too controlled to probe me for the excitement of the world outside.

"Are you not interested?" I ask.

"In what?"

"Me."

She smiles. "Should I be?"

"Yes!"

She laughs, shakes her head. "These are our treasures," she says, indicating the manuscripts. "Feel free to take one now and return it once you are done but read them with care. Keep your candles and lamps away from them, or they will go up in smoke."

∅

Later, by the light of all my candles, I peer into a manuscript. The pages are illuminated. Each image is inked with such detail, such vivid colour. One depicts two women standing naked in a green grove. Their hair is undressed, freefalling down their backs, their limbs easeful, no fear in them, and their hands extend towards each other. They are blissful and alone together. Behind the women, the night sky is lit not with stars but with luminous white leaves.

⚘ On the Subject of Short Hermitages ⚘

"Wouldn't we all like to leave our children?"

"And be fed and watered by holy hands?"

"Acting as if she was at death's door and only a few nights without sleep."

"I barely slept with my first. She didn't live a year."

"Hush, hush, neighbour. We feel your pain."

"People like Kyteler can't understand."

"One day she will."

"None escapes it. Not even the rich."

❧ May 1285 ❧

My boy and I waking, his soft body curled against mine; ablutions in the fluttering shadows of dawn; descending the stairs; watching his pottage-filled fist miss his mouth over and over, until he mastered the technique of hand entering mouth; out to the garden where he crawled after beetles and pulled himself up to stand beneath the rowan tree, toppling over, wailing, pushing himself up again; bestowing his first kiss on my mouth and another and another; planting bulbs in the ground; singing before beginning to talk; pointing at the river, the inn and me, saying "mine, mine and mine."

Now, he is two and cutting his last teeth. The hunter's. The sharpest. His cheeks are round and red with pain. I rub clove oil on his gums, and in the garden overnight freeze vegetable shavings for him to chew on.

This morning, he is busy sorting leaves and empty snail shells. But his father, who never used to come into the garden, steps out and, thoughtless, steps on the arrangement. Of course, Will cries out in frustration.

"You are disturbing him," I snap.

My husband glances at me with an expression of mildness, but no understanding.

"Let him be," I say. "I was readying to count them with him, but if you disturb him, he can't focus."

My husband frowns. "You are his mother. You don't need to teach him."

"You don't understand him." I pick Will up, but immediately he's wriggling to get down.

"He is like you," my husband says, gazing at Will who is running down the path.

He wants a boy joyless and cold like him. I see he thinks Will is too tender, too quick to cry.

Here is Will, running back to me, and he is entirely himself. He is loud, quick to laugh and loved by all who meet him. He is pleased by a bee trapped in a jug of water and screams murder when the servants try to wash him. He resembles his father only in that he was born a boy and so will have everything too easily. He will not push himself to achieve because he has no need to prove himself.

"No," I say, "he's not like me. He's like Roger."

My husband's mouth relaxes. His brother is the only person he likes, and if he thinks his son resembles Roger, rather than me, he might grow fonder of him. A child should always feel safe with their father. William's face used to light up when Roger showed him his progress in Italian and writing. I want Will to look up and see that face, and feel his father appreciates him.

Here I am pressing my cheek to Will's forehead, resting in his warmth and softness. I try to always be near him. I try to always be present. I am not like my mother. I am here for him now, always watching. He is never alone with a man, not even his father.

My husband pats Will's head, and Will meows.

My husband gives me a bewildered look, and I laugh.

"He's just a child," I say. "He wants to be a wildcat."

"He is a boy."

"He's my boy."

"You sound like an animal," my husband says.

He is on top of me. I place my wrist between my teeth. Since I gave birth to Will my husband has put himself inside me twice. On both occasions, I shamed myself by begging him. He agreed, but I felt his punishment in the way he barely touched me, finishing so swiftly I struggled to find a position where I could grow my own pleasure.

To be his wife is to be denied my animal self. It is a trial of iron and frost. He forbids me to sing in his presence and aloud wishes I would smile less. Even praying has been banned, as if he fears I have the ear of God and God might do my bidding, or perhaps he fears it is another ear I whisper to over steepled fingers. And so I live and no longer sing or smile in front of him, but life bursts on. I sing to Will. He makes me smile and smile and smile. He makes me laugh.

Daily I watch Will, and although he's all muscle and bouncing life, I am sometimes filled with dread. Even the most red-cheeked and bright-eyed farmer's children, for no reason at all, sicken and wither to be returned to the soil. I need an alternate. Just one. To quench my fear.

This the third night, I felt a need drag my insides and I reached for the only thing near, and he, cold as ever, climbed on top of me and began. Now, I try to hold the moans inside. I bite down on my skin, but they burst out, and I am rushed all over with burning pleasure. His slap sends a ringing into my head, but I am laughing. I suck in my breath, climb from under him and, singing, go behind the screen to wash. When I am dressed I will go to my workroom and put my feet up near the brazier and drink wine. I will sleep on the settle, blissfully alone, and wonder if a new life is rooting in me.

❧ The Tale of the Coin ❧

She is born in pain and fire, placed between two halves of a die and struck into being by a hammer. On her face she wears the face of a king. The minter trims her until she is round, or as close to round as his beer-numbed hand can make her. Satisfied, he tosses her, still warm, into a bag where she slips and slides against a cluster of her siblings, before lying still as if asleep.

Days later, the bag is chucked with other bags into a chest and placed on a covered cart. The horse hits the rough roads and, gleeful, the coin leaps about, clashing against the others. Finally, she is moving. Finally, something will happen to her. She knows she is destined for greatness. She overheard they are heading for the coffer of a king. A king! She will pay for his war, but perhaps, just perhaps, he will reach into her bag and pull her out from amidst the rest, select *her*. Perhaps, just perhaps, he will keep her in his breast pocket, where she will hear all the conversations of the court, and when the king is in need of guidance he will take her out and rub her between his fingertips. Soon she will be his guiding star in everything.

But her fantasies are interrupted by yells, and a dark liquid soaks her bag. It is men, chancing poor men without the power or wisdom of her king, and they are thieving her from him. She rages at the cheek of them, but she can do nothing to stop them, and she's sure: her king will have his revenge. All she must do is wait for him.

In a harbour city, she is exchanged for a cup of wine the tavern owner swears is Italian. Here, she sees all kinds of men, and none are as sweet-tempered, nor wise, as her king. One spits on her to make her shine. Another rubs her on a part of himself she wishes she had never touched. A third bites her because he says he is sure she's a fake. Yes, her!

She passes from one filthy hand to another. A boy stabs his friend and prises her from still warm fingers so he can feed his dying sister, but an old man snatches the coin from the boy's grasp and runs. The coin is worn thin by all this use and misuse. None care for her. None hold her close to their heart. She has been thumbed so often by strangers for good luck that the face of the king on her face is barely visible.

On a frozen day, a tired farmer takes her to be reminted, and the king's face emblazons her again. She dares to hope. Her wish is simpler now. It is just for a different life, a soft and easeful one where she is barely used, but the farmer soon passes her on to a wool merchant, and in his grasp she is filled with a familiar exhausted dread, but the wool merchant exchanges her, and many others minted to look like her, for a pouch of Venetian ducato. The man who now holds her in his hands is a Knight Templar, a virgin banker. She doesn't hope anything from him. She knows he will be like all the rest, but, briefly, she is pleased by him. He at least lets her rest. He locks her up in a chest beneath his floor. He writes her value onto a piece of paper, a bill of exchange, which she knows must rustle from hand to hand across Europe, perhaps passing through the fingers of many kings and queens, but none touch her, none hold her in a purse at their waist, taking her out to hold at moments of great need. No, instead she is imprisoned in the dark, without warm touch, because she, in her hard metal self, is seen as far too potent to be let out in the world. She turns men mad. She turns children into murderers. She tears families apart. Still, she waits for her day of release, because she outlives the fleshy creatures who made her. She is patient. She is full of rage now, and one day soon she will wreak her fury on her fragile makers.

❧ June 1289 ❧

Alma was sewn into her shroud this morning. I couldn't watch. I refused to attend her burial. Servants die every year, but I will never have a woman so loyal and fierce care for me again. I have lost my old angel in this world.

Now, I cannot quiet my mind. I am awaiting the return of my strongman, Felix, who has gone to foreclose on a debt. He has a subtlety to his violence. Today, he will cut off the tip of a finger from an artisan jeweller, and next week the man will find the coins he owes me. Another strongman would take too much mead and stab the debtor to death, leaving the banker with nothing but a court case from the widow.

I stop at the back door and look out at my mother's garden. I do not tend to it as I should; it has been overtaken by mint, the bushes are too large, the path clogged with weeds. Beyond the black river, there's just grey buildings and white sky. I could walk the meadows all day, collect cuckooflowers, avas and elderflowers, stow them in my basket, stop and listen to the river's song telling me what its hopes are for the sea. I could let the sun fall behind the forest before I stand to go home. I would meld into the landscape, but I stay in the city, where I am becoming wispy and unreal. Where I must diminish my voice—and myself.

On the bank of the Nore, I take off my shoes, let my bare toes curl over the edge, shut my eyes and take three deep breaths of brown river air. A barge piled with fish slides by, and the fisherman waves a mackerel at me, but I shake my head. I have my trusted fishmonger. I need no other. The water rushes loud. I feel my skin prickling against the silk of my tunic and I long to rip it off, throw it in the water and dive in after it, but I cannot float. I have never learned, and even if I had, I couldn't drift away, naked, because there are unknown eyes watching me from the inn.

Will is up near the back door, bent low in conversation with kittens. Soon they will breed, brother with sister, mother with son, in the repulsive way cats do. Soon my husband will again retreat from the inn back to his grand house, where he can breathe easy and there are no animals. It is fractious between us. I know we would be more comfortable with each other if I didn't force him to mate with me every month, but I can't stop yet. Will is six. He has passed the most dangerous winters of his life, but still. Still.

Down here by the water, there is only me. I hear crackling in my ears like flames inside my head. I hear Will yelling—he's been scratched by a kitten—and then, for no reason at all, everything is changed. Yellow air drifts aslant. I see the river and the rowan tree as if through amber and I know, somehow, I am pregnant with a daughter. I have never known anything uncertain before, but this I am sure of. She is nested high in my body, pressing against my ribs, as if she's already trying to break out of me and fly into the sky. And I too want to spread out my arms, reach into this yellow day and take flight. I am airy with the thought of her. A daughter. A girl like me.

🌿 Shrovetide 1290 🌿

Forty days of Lent. Forty days of mere bread and fish. I chew mint to numb the sensation of starvation and crunch ice, but I fear if I don't eat flesh and sweets my daughter will start to eat me from the inside out.

I feel the moon rise inside me and I think of my mother. The wind and the trees were always calling her away from me, but I won't allow myself to be called away from Will nor the daughter inside me. I am here in Kilkenny for them.

Will finds me drizzling honey on my bread. I give him a piece and press my finger to my lips. He nods and licks a dribble off his thumb. I have an ally, but my pangs of hunger fail to retreat. The babe has consumed all the sweetness, and I am left ravenous still.

I have at least four weeks before the birth, but I am prepared. I have placed four jars of wine beneath my bed, and inside my wooden chest is a small, stoppered bottle to numb my spine. These will only take the corners off my agony. What folly to invite a man between my legs. My life is precious to me. It feels more precious each day. Will needs me. I will never reach for my husband again, and despite the weight of the baby, this thought makes me feel light.

The baby hasn't moved all day.

Two days. Two nights. In my belly, a deathly stillness. I pace the inn's rooms. I pace the garden. Beneath my foot, a crunch. A crushed snail. Far off, crows shriek and tumble against splintering grey clouds. The baby is dead, I know it. I must get it out. The longer I carry it, the more likely it is to kill me too.

At the end of my bed is my mother's wooden chest. The bottle I need is small. Mother told me she never used it herself, but she gave it to the servants. It's a hazard of working at an inn to often fall pregnant—always a randy merchant or a bored monk lurking. The dark liquid was made many moons ago when I was just a girl, but poison doesn't age. I measure out a spoon, swallow it before a thought of danger can surface and stop me.

Pain shoots through my spine and into my mind. I think about my husband's weak body, of late his incessant reasonableness, his incessant ageing.

"William!"

My daughter will not live. She won't ever see a sunset.

She is furry like all baby animals. I lick her head, and it tastes of salt and sweet.

She mewls, not for milk but for an end to her tiny torment. I am selfish and won't hand her to the wet nurse. I cannot let her go. I watch and watch each breath. I hate the gaps in between. They leave me hanging in fear, waiting for the puny inhale.

She is ugly. Not like Will who came out round and red and screaming. She is pale and scrawny, all sharp angles and a bulbous head. She is not what a baby girl ought to be. I was beautiful even as a babe, Father told me so, but my daughter will never be beautiful. This shouldn't matter if she is soon to be dead, but I want her to rival the angels. In death, I want her loved better than any of the other uncountable lost infants.

She is floppy. She sleeps on and on. The wet nurse takes her, my hands too slow to snatch her back, and pinches her at each hour of the bell.

I want my daughter to open her eyelids and show me her eyes are as green as the river, but I must push her lids open myself, and like every other newborn, her sightless gaze is blue.

I send her away with the wet nurse for I cannot bear to hear her tiny, strangled breaths. I cannot bear to see her tiny, wrinkled face.

I wait all day for the message to come: she is dead.

My eyelids break open. White light. Blinding until I see. William stands over me. The baby is flopped against one arm. As if it were any other day, he doesn't look at me.

He is smiling down at her.

The room smells of rotten apples.

She is so tiny.

I pinch the back of my hand.

He names her Rose. He is a fool. She will never see the buds bloom pink. She will never see the summer.

.   .   .

I toss and turn and do not sleep. My mind flits. Next to me, he is still.

I was so sure I did right to drink the poison. I was sure she was dead.

A fly slams against the walls of my workroom, trying for its freedom.

Coins, coins, I count coins.

The fly has stopped its slamming. If I go searching for it, I am sure I will find it a husk.

A servant interrupts me often.

At dawn:

"Mistress, won't you step out into the garden where it's fresher? It smells like an animal's died in here."

At sext:

"I have left you a plate of food. It'll attract the mice if you don't eat it."

Dusk:

"Your washing water is hot now . . . I don't wish to waste it on a child, but young Will may have it if you do not. Mistress?"

Witching hour:

"Try to sleep. Please?"

My husband sends the servant with reports:

The babe wakes sometimes and searches for the wet nurse's breast.

The babe's finally uncurled her fists so the crust stuck between her fingers can be washed away.

The babe's voice is still not strong enough to cry beyond a bleat.

The babe's face has smoothed, and she is become prettier.

. . .

I go to see her at prime. I stand in the kitchen doorway. It is all a-clatter in there. Cook and the serving girl give their nods and get back to shaving parsnips for the morning meal. The wet nurse has her back to me and with one hand shovels spoonfuls of pottage from an enormous bowl into her mouth. I glance about, searching for my daughter. The wet nurse turns, calling for more food, and I see the tiny head in the crook of her arm. The eyes are shut again.

Lying in the bed, my husband's eyes are open, fixed on the ceiling, and for a moment I think he is dead, but he sits up.

"You won't ask me then?" I say.

He pulls his tunic over his head, and it settles around his body. He looks up, smooths the fabric against his chest and places a hand on my arm.

"I wanted to speak of what I did to our daughter," I say.

His hand falls. "She's living."

"You don't wonder why she was born early?"

"Such occurrences are common."

I push up the smile I use for all men, and some women, which makes sweet young monks beg me to end their celibacy and send them to Hell.

"Alice." He sighs and gives me his forbearing look. I've seen him bestow it on Will when my tender-hearted boy gives a coin to a man crippled by the wars with the Gaels.

"You mustn't blame yourself," my husband says.

He pats my shoulder and, shaking his head, leaves me alone.

I put my hand on the door of the wet nurse's little room, but I hear a man's voice, humming. William is singing to our daughter. I never knew he could sing.

"The baby is the servants' concern," I declare to my husband.

The dining hall is full of rowdy guests: four monks, a wine merchant and his family of several children. All are caught up in their own conversations and don't look at me, despite how loud my voice seems to be.

He puts down his knife, stands and strides out of the room.

I push my plate away. A monk with a wet nose is watching me.

"Alice? Sleep. Please, just sleep."

"She's dead."

Will is standing in the doorway of my workroom, holding something small in his hands.

I rush around my table, cross the room and grab his hands. He is holding a small grey kitten.

"Mama?" he says. "Shall I feed her to the dogs?"

My hand slams across his face. Sobbing, he runs from the room, the dead kitten clutched to his chest.

"Just hold her," he says.

"Just watch her," he says.

"Here's Rose. Just pat her back."

"Just rock her."

"She's just fallen asleep."

"She's just a baby."

"She's your baby."

"Just, please."

❧ Outside the Meat Seller's ❧

"Afraid of her own baby."

"Haven't you seen the face on it?"

"If it were mine, I'd leave it out in the snow."

"I heard he doesn't lie with her."

"So it's a demon's child?"

"It's the only explanation."

A Dreamed-of Daughter

In the beginning, she is a pink ball curled up in my arms, unfurling, blossoming into a girl with flaming eyebrows which I must pluck. I wash her face in milk each morning and after, at the garden door, she feeds it to the cats. Her laugh is quick and sometimes spiteful. Swiftly, she understands more than most grown men about money and fabric and conversation. Sure, she lacks her brother's ease and sweetness, but she has grit and perseverance. This is how a girl is made different to a boy. She either fights or is swallowed. My dreamed-of daughter fights. She never marries. She has no use for men.

❧ Rose ❧

My daughter and I are separate. She has left purple stripes across my belly. Her body flops, still, as if she were a babe, but she is not. She must be carried everywhere by servants or even me. Still, at two years old, she has almost no hair. The wisps are as pale as her father's. She shivers in the draughts only she can feel. Her eyes are too enormous. They are as green as mine and they watch me, asking questions I don't want to answer: Please, can you stop working and pick me up now? Will you hold me on your lap and stroke my head? How many days do I have left now? When? When will you leave me? Please, don't leave me.

Often I give in, run to her, hold her, whisper words I don't think she can understand. Often I send for a servant, so I don't have to see her eyes begging.

❧ September 1292 ❧

Crows are circling the roof of St. Mary's church, calling, calling out their calamitous sounds.

Will strides through the grass, skipping over graves. He turns, stretches his arms above his head and yawns vastly.

"Did you know bees make their homes out of wax?" he says.

"I did."

"And the queens eat their husbands."

"Who told you that?"

"Roger," he says. "But you're not going to believe this, Mother: it's only after the men bees give them babies."

"Shocking." I laugh.

"We're going to have a hive in the garden."

"There." I point at a gravestone carved with a cross and decorated with ornate, twirling lines. "That's my father's."

Will drapes an arm over it and bends to read. He counts on his fingers.

"Twelve years dead," he says.

"It doesn't feel so long."

"Was he like me?" he asks.

"Yes. Almost everyone liked him."

"Father doesn't like me. He's always patient with Rose, but never with me."

I mean to tell him he's right, his father doesn't like him, but he shouldn't care as he will still inherit, and anyway I like him better than anyone in the world, but he is sprinting towards the church doors, whooping. Always, he seems to race away from difficulty like a swallow leaving Ireland ahead of the snow. He is one for joy, not one to linger on what could make him sorrowful. I love this about him, but these last few years I have watched Will wince each time his father criticises his uneven writing or his labouring too long over a calculation. Daily, Will runs to me to ask the solution to some business problem his father has posed for him, and I am pulled away from my task to sit with him and discuss it, but usually he reaches a sound conclusion with only a little nudging. I have watched as he tenses in his father's presence. I have watched him race out the door with Roger, who invites Will to accompany him when he attends the council. I have watched Will weep on the stairs and held him while he told me he was simpleminded, and, vehemently, I said he was brighter than most men, but not all skill lies in a ledger; most is in dealing with people, and I have never seen anyone extract smiles as expertly as him. I felt his body shake against me. I felt his disbelief, but also his hope.

Now, he bounds back across the graveyard to me.

"Don't worry," he says, "I'll look after Rose when you're dead."

I smile and say thank you, and he, like a sparrow, puts his head on one side, curious and suspicious all at once. He knows my face better than anyone. He knows I'm not saying what I feel. He knows I came here to talk, but he doesn't know what I wanted to say.

"Has your father ever looked at you strangely?" I ask.

"You've asked me that before, Mother," he says. "I know what to look for, but he's not like that. Not with me."

"Good, but if that ever changes—"

"I know, I know."

Somewhere near, I can smell thatch burning. Screams faint on the air. Nothing uncommon in a business or a home vanishing to flames. Nothing uncommon in people dying, but still.

"Home?" he says.

"Home," I say.

I grab his hand, and together we run.

⌀

I stride towards the rowan, my daughter resting against my shoulder and Will rushing ahead, calling to the servants who run with buckets up and down to the river. There is smoke in the air. A butcher's is alight. The smell of sizzling fat hangs all about. I yell at the servants to ignore the inn for now, to run to the meat shop and throw their water on the blaze. Far wiser to stop the fire spreading at the source than waiting for it to reach us.

Will leaps onto the path as if he wants to go with them, but I whistle to him. His shoulders slump, but he comes back to me.

I lay Rose on my mantle beneath the rowan tree.

"You'll be safe here," I whisper. "Rowans protect from fire."

She gazes up at the branches. I lie down beside her, nestle her head in the curve of my armpit. Above us, the berries hang in heavy red clusters. The dark leaves wave. Softly, I hum an old tune, pulled from the depths of myself, forgotten until now, my mother's or perhaps Alma's lullaby. Rose is cracked open by music. Every week I employ a flautist to play for her, and she bobs about to his tunes, mouth open, smiling, still toothless, still. I have never felt so afraid as when I look at my daughter dancing. I don't look down at her now, but I feel her head gently nodding in discordant rhythm with my voice.

"Mother." Will is standing over us, his eyes alight with the thrill that possesses some children. "Have you ever killed someone?"

"Come here," I say, opening my free arm to him. "Lie down."

He throws himself beside me. His body scatters heat, while hers emits cold. I press myself firmer against her. I am trying to hold on. I am trying to preserve them both. I send out a silent prayer to my mother, to her tree. Please, continue breathing life between my children's lips. Just, please.

❧ November 1293 ❧

I have felt that angel treading behind me, black wings sharpened in judgement at what I did to her, how I wanted her gone from my body, how I feared her from birth, but now I am calm. The angel of death has retreated—perhaps they have stopped to torment some other mother for a day or two—and I am ensconced in my work-room with James Powers. He draws the purse strings and solicits loans across Europe for the impoverished crown. It is many years since we danced at my May party, and I lost my chance with him to birthing Will, but now I have regained the opportunity I mean to seize it. Tonight is All Saints' Eve, and we have retreated from the churchmen eagerly gathering the sins of the living who weep for the dead. It would be a waste to join them. I don't wish to speak with the dead. I am here for the living. I am here for Will and Rose. I need to know if I ever vanish from their world, my son will be free to protect her, and freedom in this city is bought. Edward, the beggar king, will never repay me any loan. None of his lenders will ever recoup their coins, but if I give him what he wants, make this stake in the trade routes for my wool investments into England, make contact with all the women and men in his court, I will make an enormous, if circuitous, profit.

I pour Powers another tumbler of my best French wine, and he eases back in the settle, glancing pleasantly about the room, taking in my father's tapestries, the woods and the wild beasts, the flowers and the sharpened spears. He smiles, yawns, downs his wine in two neat gulps and places the tumbler on my table. He is a repellent man but dressed in fine-spun wools of tasteful, deep dyes. His nose is extraordinary, so large that even from where I sit behind the table I can see the shadow darken half his face. I place my wine down. There's no need to pretend to drink because his eyes are no longer on me. He is easing into the space, relaxing, his mind ready for bending in whichever direction I choose.

I am about to speak when a new draught invades the workroom. My husband enters, empty-handed, no rings, no gloves, no purse. He eddies towards my guest, and I can see words brimming in him, but he doesn't speak them. He's storing them up, and so they must be poisonous. They will ruin my deal before it has fully begun.

"Husband," I say. "You know Powers."

Powers straightens, planting his feet more firmly on the floor, readying to stand.

"Don't get up," I tell him. "My husband didn't mean to interrupt us."

"Your wife is forceful in her instruction," Powers says, remaining seated. "I find I cannot refuse her."

My husband wears deep lines around his mouth. He is staring at my guest with an almost malicious look, but he has never once been covetous of me. It is some other wind that's shifted his usual stillness into what almost reads to me as frustration on his tight lips.

I stride around the table and take his arm.

"If it's so important," I say, "I will step into the hall with you."

"No." He removes my hand from his arm. "I don't wish to offend you," he says to Powers.

"I am to be disappointed then." Powers smiles.

"My wife will not listen to reason, at least not from me. I put it to you to convince her that lending to your friend would be a grave mistake."

Powers nods at his hands which sit neatly piled in his lap. With his right thumb and index finger, he turns a ring on his left hand. He is steady. The king's trust is well placed.

"I'll leave you two to discuss this yourselves," Powers says. "Far be it for me to get between a lady and her spouse."

He stands up, bows slightly to William, his half-grin toothy and sharp.

"Mistress Outlaw," he says, "I shall drop in again before my departure from Kilkenny."

In the doorway, Will stands, holding his sister.

"Yours?" Powers turns back to me, his lips curling, finally an expression of vague irritation. My family has intruded with too much reality. The fantasy I've built of alluring banker woman is broken.

I nod but say nothing, because he knows they are my children.

"See you, Powers." Will, guileless as ever, smiles at England's most influential man. We hear the voice of a servant in the hall bidding Powers to take it safely on the roads to the castle. The street door closes.

My husband lifts Rose from Will's arms.

"How dare you," I say.

He looks wearily beyond me at nothing at all. I rest my hand briefly on Rose's damp cheek, but my husband moves out of my reach, Rose nestling her head against his neck.

He climbs the stairs and I watch her small white head peeking over his shoulder.

"Another winter is coming," I call.

He pauses. "And?"

And, I don't say a word. I don't say at night I stand over her bed with a feather to watch her laboured, erratic breaths. I don't say each summer she lives I fear the coming winter will take her. I don't say anything, but I feel my son take my hand and squeeze it, and I sink slowly towards him, hold his warm body against mine.

"And winter is coming," I say to my husband's retreating back.

He freezes, but only momentarily, before climbing the last few steps and vanishing with her.

❦

I step over the body of the boy outside my daughter's door. His hand clutches the knife, forged to protect her.

Her room is cold, but in her bed my daughter is too warm, heated by the servant girl beside her. Everyone is abandoning her for sleep, but I will not.

This room was mine once. Now it is hers. It was a safe place. That's why I chose to put her here. She is still so small. Her sharp elbow pokes out from the blankets. I kneel beside her pallet, put the lamp on the floor. Slowly, I place my hand on her tiny fragile chest; her skin is clammy, but there it is, her fractured breath. She mumbles words in her own language. I have never spoken with her, not like Will and my husband do, telling her about their lives while she listens, her eyes wide and brimming with adoration. I am not like them. I have never known how to gaze long into her eyes, sharing myself. I have never known how to stand inside the pain of losing her.

I slip a hand beneath her neck, and the other under her legs, and lift her into my arms. Gently, I cling to her. She moans, and I feel her moan lodge in the back of my own throat like a shard of ice. I place my hand on the flame of the lamp. I need to shock out of myself. I can't really be here. My hand is searing pain. Loudly, she is moaning, but no. She's not. It's me.

❧ January 1294 ❧

My daughter is dying this night.

The buildings, the road, the sky are all black. These familiar places have turned strange in their nightly shapes. I am dressed in my red cloak, a flame in the night's cold. Dark falls fast as I walk towards home. Street bonfires are blazing like roses blooming against the white snow. My gloves are solid, stuck to the handle of my lamp. I stop at the city gates, tempting the nightwatchmen to threaten me with a beating for breaking the curfew, but they don't turn to look at me. My lantern has gone out.

❧

I find the dining hall unlit and echoey, the kitchen empty, all the servants asleep or hidden. I step into my mother's garden, stride down the path to her tree. At the water's edge, I drop my dead lantern. I never asked my mother if she lost babes before I was born. Perhaps they had names. Perhaps she sang songs for them, still in her womb. I never asked how she kept moving and speaking and being.

Inside the inn, the women begin to keen. My scream sounds like a wild thing tethered. There is a movement in the air over the river, a rush of white feathers in the dark. I reach over the water. It's her I'm after. My daughter. It's Hell or Heaven or that place in between, but it's all the same. It's all death.

White feathers float against black.

∅

I can't go to her room. I wait for the inn to move again as it always does; but when it does, I cannot bear the clatter of pewter plates, the whispers, the hush of shoes on the rush-covered floors. Worst are the prickly silences. I must stay. I stay in the garden, stand beneath the eaves as the rain blasts down. Ahead of me, in the mud, puddles reflect a black and white sky.

The garden door swings wide, but I don't look to see who opened it. I know it's him. No one else would dare come near me on this day.

"I can't have her buried," I say. "Her chest is too weak. Under the soil she won't be able to draw a breath. Let's leave her down by the river, or if we must bury her, then let it be here in the garden. She wouldn't be alone then."

I look at him and see one grey tear is caught in his bottom lashes. I touch my cheeks, but they are dry.

"Heresy," he says.

He thinks me mad, but if madness is losing a child, then he too is mad.

✤ A Letter to a Lady ✤

Dear Lady,

I don't want to presume by taking up much of your day reading, but I needed to send you my condolences. We have not spoken much, which I regret. What I mean to say is when I was a boy, I lost my sister. She was almost three. Nothing is worse than a child flying from you too soon. It is always too soon.

I wish to tell you, I cannot know what you suffer. I cannot imagine, but I hope you're not alone. I hope you weep in company. I hope you know she is in a better place. I hope one day this will ease your pain.

I know you are a woman of great feeling. I sense this must make the pain near unbearable. Please, hold on. They say the passing days and years ease the agony of loss. This I have not found to be true, but as the years go on, we can, I feel, become used to pain.

Please tell your son and husband I am grieved for them. A child. A sister. Nothing is worse. You are all in my thoughts.

Richard de Valle

❧ June 1294 ❦

Most nights I dream the garden is choked with roses. They grow over the inn and snake through the doors, pricking me as I pass. Droplets of blood litter the floorboards and stone paving. There is blood in the beds and in the food.

I wake, and my mouth tastes as if I've bitten down on a knife. My husband's hands stroke my neck, clamp and gently tighten. He knows I didn't want the burden of being her mother. This betrayal of her, my shame has seeped out of me, and even he, as dense as he is, has realised I am to blame for our daughter's death.

I do not fight his fingers, once so slippery, now rough. I lie still, eyes wide, gazing at the shadowness of him in the lamplight. I think this is how my mother died, with the hands of her husband tightening around her neck. I think of Will, his sister dead, his mother dead, and I buck against my husband. I claw at his face, pushing him away with all my force, and he lets go, drags himself off me. I am left gasping, grappling for a hold of something, anything in the dark.

At last, I lie still and think I hear my husband weeping.

❧ Lament ❧

Sung by Three Mothers

She lies on stone dreaming
ice-fingered visions of demons
dancing; kissing; laughing; sinning.
Still, she is unrepentant
but weeps on bent knee,
pressing ardent kisses
to the Devil's mouth.
All to escape the righteous
holy fires, but no words
will save her from damnation.
No sandbags at the door,
no rowan in full bud can keep green life
inside her foul offspring. Even in sleep,
her greedy fingers clutch her purse,
her jewels and ointment pipe.
She wakes and knows it's over.
Already, she is burning.

❧ August 1294 ❧

It's late evening. Brambles and grasses spear the garden's soil and smother the softer plants. Instead of reaching heavenwards, the pea shoots lie against the ground, and the kale is thick and wild. I pierce the earth with a naked toe, my nail slicing. Roger charges down the path, his cloak banging herbs, releasing the scent of rosemary and marjoram.

"Alice." He takes my hand and leads me away from the inn, stopping only when we're beneath the rowan. He smells of the open road and the open sky. The day is darkening, but it is not yet terce. All, it seems, is coming to an end.

"As a girl," I say, "I dreamed of the forest. Now I dream not at all. I never asked her what she dreamed. Her eyes would've told me if I'd paused to look long enough. Those eyes. If you had married me, she never would've been born. She never would have died."

His arms reach around me. I cling to him, soak in his warmth, press my cheek against the firmness of his chest.

"Don't move," I say.

My hand is on my belly. It is empty, emptier than it has ever been, sagging, loose, useless. Beyond the garden walls lightning slams down. I sense it blasts through the forest, splitting trees open and leaving them gaping and burning.

I reach for my wimple and pull it back.

"Don't." He sounds so very sad.

I untie each rope of my hair and run my fingers through it. It sways about me, reaching almost to my knees. He is still here, watching, watching my hair which appears dark in the fading light, but he must know it is red. I am waiting for another lightning strike so I might be illuminated, but none comes, and I am drenched, my hair already blackened with water. It's too late for him to see me.

"Please." I don't know if it's him or me who speaks. I do know he doesn't want me; he never has. I watch him, a blurry shadow, stride away, and I am gasping, as if for my final breath, but still I live within the gasps, the panic rising and falling. In the struggle I welcome death. In death there would be nothing, or perhaps two things better than nothing: my mother; my daughter.

*

At night, in the kitchen, I slice off my hair with a meat knife.

❧ War ❧

"Our bellies ache."

"Selfish bastards. Why can't the
lordships be content? They're rolling
in coin, but they make us fight each
other to fill their coffers to bursting."

"We do it all for you, our dear
peasant workers. You must
know, we only have Ireland's best
interests at heart."

"Are you listening? We're starving."

"Now the Gaels are killing us. All
we want is an easy life, but that's
too much to ask from our lords."

"We don't appreciate your tone.
Don't you know all of you are
easily replaced?"

"All we wanted was to feed our babies.
All we wanted was our freedom.
You left us no choice.
We'll kill you all.
Or die trying."

❧ July 1295 ❧

I should have known a meadow is never silent. No, it is loud with summer, grasshoppers purring, sheep coughing and the river crashing. I feel the sting of the nettle, the bite of the wasp, the softness of iris petals. I am standing on the riverbank, dipping a willow branch in the water. At my feet are foxgloves, gently holding back their poison. Above me, there is a shifting in the air, a wingbeat of a bird silently passing overhead. A pair of crows try to land in the top branches of a hawthorn, shrieking, bursting back into the air as their claws meet thorns.

The sky is heavy with heat. I shiver with a strange and fearful knowing. The light dips away from the road and races across the meadow, over me, brushing the river and vanishing. I hear the wind before it reaches me. The air tastes brittle, and I am pincered with sharp rain. My purse bangs hot against my leg. My skin itches. I smell dirt. I smell tar. In my hand I hold a burning branch. I blink and blink. Did I set it on fire? But now I can't see it. All is white, now red, now black. I run, run for where I remember the river. I sniff for water, but all I can smell is singed flesh. I keep running. I barely feel the ground beneath my feet. The slam of cold river water is a shuddering shock to my head and eyes and teeth. I force my body down. My chest feels like it's collapsing, but I fight to stay beneath until the noise of water shrieking in my ears is so unbearable I must burst out again. Everything is too sharp and bright. I can't make out the meadow. I see a pale orb like a lantern, but it breaks into many shining stars. I push myself under the water again, feel the pressure over my head and on my neck. My chest wants to scream with the pain, but I stay down to smell her head, to taste her breath, to see her eyes, too large, just once, Rose, gazing back at me.

I burst up. The bank is all sharp lines. It's all black and white, and barely any shades of grey.

"Fuck!" I try to push under again, but I can't.

"What a mouth you have," a man's voice calls.

"Who's there?"

A smudge of a figure approaches me. A shepherd perhaps. No one else would be out here. Not when the fighting is so close. Not in the midst of a storm.

There's a thunder clap behind me. I feel his hands on mine, dragging me. My sight is still full of sparks. I feel the sharp stalks of grass on my fingertips and the incline of the hill under my bare feet.

"I lost my shoes in the river," I say.

"They were blown off when the lightning struck you. They'll be somewhere in the grass if they've not burned."

Struck by lightning. I was struck by lightning.

"You were burning," he says. "It's lucky you were so close to the river. Lucky you jumped in."

The wind is roaring, and I begin to feel a terrible cold. We walk a long way. I grip his hand. Somehow, I am not afraid. My mind whirrs ahead of me. What if this blindness is permanent? I will have to hire a man to bring me around. I will have to get my man to read out my ledger every morning. What men will agree to hand over their money to a woman who cannot see to count it? I shut my eyelids tight, shake my head and open them again, and the white smudges have shrunk a little. The brightness is less sharp. There is hope.

I grip his hand tighter. His arm brushing mine is hard, jolts pain up my shoulder. There are pine needles and damp leaves under my feet now. I sense the tree trunks close by. I put out my free hand and take a few steps until my palm connects with bark and I can lean against the tree and smell rain on green and hear the thunder tumbling away towards Kilkenny.

"Here." His hands brush my skin as he places something heavy on my shoulders. Fur tickles the back of my neck and cheek. No, this is no shepherd's cheap wool cloak, but I know the voice of every wealthy man in Kilkenny and beyond. Yet he is a stranger to me.

"I know you," I say.

"You don't know me."

His breath is aniseed and sandalwood. Like me, he flavours himself with spices from faraway countries.

"Do you have a death wish?" I can hear a smile in his voice. He's teasing.

"Perhaps I enjoy living on the edge."

"You wander out alone when Gaels—worse, our own soldiers—are rumoured to be roaming near here."

My teeth are chattering, but I say, "I do not fear men."

He laughs. "I can see that. I'll go and tell the watchman to send your servant."

"No. You can't leave me here." I grasp for his hands but cannot find them. "You must take me back."

"You, a woman unafraid of men, you'll be fine. Anyway, you wouldn't want to walk into town, your clothes half burnt from your body, with me, a stranger leading you. What would people say?"

"I barely care."

He laughs. "Well, pity me at least." His voice is already receding. "I have my own reputation to protect," he's shouting now. "One day, I'll come to your inn to collect my cloak."

He knows me.

"I'll have sold it if you take too long," I yell.

His laugh is far off, yet it shatters me as if the lightning had turned me to glass. The world now is too visible. Kilkenny, a grey mass in the distance, and him, a small figure crossing the ditch from meadow to road. The sun strikes down from between matted clouds and his head is set alight.

It was Will who named him for me.

We were at the market, browsing fruit, when I caught sight of a red beard.

"That's Adam le Blund." I tried to catch hold of each word . . . Adam! (what a name!) . . . hails from Callan . . . a merchant . . . a lender . . . I am watching Adam's mouth speaking, his hands animating his words in a wild and virile manner. Hanging near him was a soppy, freckled wife and too many girls to count.

He gave me a broad smile, a knowing smile. I walked home with two thoughts. He remembers me. He wants me.

*

Five summers in a row he comes to Kilkenny. The sun rises, and there he is, but never, never once does he stay at my inn. Never does he let me brush by him in the corridor and breathe in his scent of horse or beer or sweat. Never does he give me the chance to become like all the men I despise, cornering him, whispering vile or beautiful words into his empty ear. At least not yet.

*

Adam. He is the man all men ought to be replicated from. Bright, laughing blue or grey eyes—I never get close enough to know for sure. Hair, if you touched it, that would set you on fire. Shoulders broad and rounded. All muscle. Torso broad. A lifetime of eating good meat. Stance always wide as if he's just leapt off his horse and is still becoming accustomed to walking.

Adam. The maker of daughters.

Adam.

*

He was made from God's own finger and led to the one forbidden tree by her. But I am not her. I am his superior. I am Lilith, made too from God's own flesh. I am known for my friendship with wildcats and the goatman. I am known for hatching eggs and, like a tree, gathering birds under her shadow.

I was made to be his hunter, but like me he enjoys the hunt. He teases me with those laughing eyes, licking his lips when he sees me, touching his brow as if he is bashful beneath my gaze. He knows I hunger for him. He drives me wild on purpose. I don't know what I will do.

*

He is my poison and remedy. My distraction. I fill myself with thoughts of him, and the heaviness inside me flits away to hide in a dark corner.

❧ February 1301 ❧

"Remember," the priest says, aloft his pulpit, "man thou art dust and to dust thou shalt return."

My muscles are screaming. The lightning is in my body still, smashing like a terrible bell against my bones. All along my left arm the scars form a trunk, and over my shoulder and across my chest they are white tangled branches on a winter tree. Some nights now, I am hit with terrific hope. I think of Adam whose strong hands led me to the forest. Adam with his flaming hair and wicked smile. I think of us standing on the forest's edge, on the edge of something free.

Some days, from nowhere I am hit with terror. I hear a shrieking inside my head. My foot turns numb, my mouth tastes of burnt iron, and nested in me is a secret wish, a precious white flame in a dark cave, passionate and painful. I wish to stab out the eyes of the men always watching, le Poer most of all. I wish I was no longer wed, my husband dead. I wish myself alone in a wild place.

The priest approaches his congregation, all obediently bowing their heads. He splashes me with bitter water and smudges ash upon my forehead. This is the message: soon you will be ash; soon you shall burn.

Beside me, my husband looks at me from beneath his thin eyelids and says, "Alice." Just that, but my name on his lips sounds strange. My tunic is tightening around my neck. There is a massive lump inside my throat, sharp as splintered ice. My chest is on fire, and I cannot breathe. I fear I am dying, but I am trying to live. I try to scream, but no sound comes out.

❧ On the Guildhall Steps ❧

"Old Outlaw . . ."

"He's shrunken and grey."

"Like a year-old carrot."

"On the way out."

"That wife of his . . ."

"She's a dragon."

"When she looks at me, I piss myself."

"Once he's gone . . ."

"She'll be wanting another man in her bed."

"Le Poer, he's the hungriest."

"Shame his wife is still living."

"Don't forget Kyteler's husband."

❧ The Bed ❧

When my marriage bed was made, it was carried, for all to see, through the streets of Kilkenny. The posts were carved with the leaves and flowers of an oak, but it was hewn from a yew, the eternal tree, the poisoner, masked as the king of the forest.

It is simply a bed, but when I was twelve, my father told me beds are where we make children, but I knew beds are also where children can be unmade, where a man's force can dislodge them, before they have rooted strongly enough. In the safety of our beds we are meant to mould our dreams. Yet beds can be places where a child is forced to no longer be a child.

I know that, in my father's bed, my mother's nights were as white as mine. White with the need to run.

❧ May 1301 ❧

Much is rare this evening. We rarely retire together. We rarely walk side by side up the stairs to our bed. We move with exaggerated care. We take off our outer wool cyclas and our shoes and climb into bed. In the white night, a cat hisses, spits, yawls. There's a splattering sound and the scent of sour meat.

My husband and I stay awake sensing each other's tiniest movements. We hear the shriek of silence. We lie side by side. We have reached the witching hour. The inn rustles. Servants and guests wake to fumble beneath their blankets, reaching for whatever soft flesh is nearest.

I am rocking back and forth, panicked but focused on each new breath and him here, beside me, sleeping or awake, breathing soft, uneven, perhaps he's dreaming. I cannot breathe, but now, at last, I'm not alone because he cannot breathe either. I hold the pillow over his face. Like all the lovers in the rooms around us, our bodies struggle against each other, desperate, needy of life. My fingers ache from gripping. I release my hold on the pillow. His body lies still, warm and soft beneath me. I am breathing with ease again. I am light as a girl running in the meadow.

🌿 Graveside Whispers 🌿

"Laughing, she was. The next morning too."

"Just like her father."

"Servants found him with a cat on his chest."

"Purring."

"Brutal. I've always said it. The whole family."

"He's penniless now."

"We're all penniless in the grave."

❧ May 1301 ❧

My husband is dead, and I feel a bright sense of treason. My hands hang empty at my sides. Such strength lay dormant in each finger, power enough to silence a man. Looking at them, slender and ink-stained, I know them to be mine, yet they are a marvel. I ought to feel a weight of shame upon my head. I ought to feel angels' tears falling on my face, but I feel nothing except relief.

Will stands beside me, his arm heavy over my shoulder, his chin resting on the top of my head. Our backs are to the garden, but I can smell it. Already the first roses are blowing in the breeze. The herbs explode over the paths. The garden is offensively alive, reminding us again: he is dead. We stare at the inn, smoke spiralling up from the chimneys. We honour him for a moment, just us two.

"I would have done the same," he says.

"Don't tell Roger."

His laugh is cold and bright. He too watched his uncle at the burial weep in the sight of all Kilkenny. Roger could never imagine what I have done. Not even the whisperers could convince him. He would only believe it from our own lips.

I wrap my arms around Will and squeeze. He is a man now, but he is mine still. He has always been entirely mine. I take a deep breath and laugh.

❧ June 1301 ❧

I am alone. Will has left me. He's moved into his father's old house. All these years, I've longed for him to be safe and grown, but now he's breaking free, I want more than anything to pull him back, make him return to boyhood, but we are both grown now. He has stepped into his own life.

Standing in my inn's hallway, I am aware everything here will outlive me. These stairs, every stool and piss pot, even this dusty air I breathe; but there, beyond the dining-hall door, light shines warm and beckoning. Until the end, I will fill this inn with life.

In the heat and clamour of the party, I watch Adam le Blund's wife. She is pretty in a pale and simple way. Her forehead is fashionably high and pink from plucking. Her face is drowning in an intensely starched wimple. I never would have imagined such a small and frail woman birthing so many children—and already she is bulbous with another. She wears many guises: the tender-hearted wife stroking his arm as she hands him a cup of wine; the doting mother leading her daughters, who range in age from twelve to perhaps eighteen, about the room so unwed men might admire them; the convivial traveller nodding as the old merchants' wives prattle away to her; the trusting lover who retires from the party early, leaving her husband alone and unattended.

This is when his gaze finally rests on me, and we smile and smile.

We smile because we know we want each other, and yet we know it is forbidden, and this makes our smiles grow so vast they hurt our faces. Half the room must have noticed the heat between us by now, but I don't care. I have drunk too much wine. I long to float to him, to hotly drag him from the room and, in the shadows of the hall, just out of sight of my neighbours but still close enough to cause me a thrill of fear, press my mouth to his chest.

"I must leave you," a voice says just behind me. I turn and find it's de Valle. Sweet, gentle de Valle.

"Thank you for a wonderful evening." His hands are fidgeting with his gloves, his eyes cast down.

"Won't you stay a little longer?" I ask. "I never get to talk to you."

He looks into my face now, seeming to search me, and I think I must be blushing, or perhaps it's just the heat of the room. "You are far too busy with more important people than me. I wish you goodnight."

He draws his hand away, bows and retreats from me, his grey eyes so very sad, and once he's gone, I am left standing in the centre of my dining hall, alone and holding a hollow feeling in my chest.

"De Valle's wife died three years ago." Boldly, Will grins at me. "Think of all his coin, his land. The title."

"He's too quiet."

"He's nothing like Father."

"I can't be with a timid man."

"De Valle isn't timid. He's—"

"Did you hear Adam le Blund singing earlier? He has a powerful strong voice."

"Oh, he's a one. Now, come with me."

"No." I gaze about the room, but I can't find Adam. He has left without a word, or even a glance.

"You don't need me, do you?" I say.

"Of course I do," he says.

Will takes my arm and guides me through the thinning crowd, into the hall and up the stairs.

I seem to blink, and we are in my bedchamber. He is pulling back my blankets, taking off my shoes and handing me into bed. In the half-light, I gaze at my boy who is no longer a boy. He presses a kiss to my forehead and quietly withdraws from the room, leaving me heavy with the need to weep.

*

Adam le Blund stands far enough back from where I sit at my counting table so I can view his entire body: the thick growth of his red beard, the arch smile, the rounded muscles of his legs beneath his purple tunic. In this rare stillness, I see vividly his good humour and speed all vibrating beneath his surface, ready to break out at any moment, and he does; he strides into the room, leaving the door wide open.

I sniff as if I am mildly bored, but he grins as he looks about the workroom. My head is banging with the remnants of last night's drinking, but I slept long and dreamed of nothing at all. What release it was to be emptied of all images, all senses, to sink into the nothing, if only briefly. Now, as I gaze at him, he, in all his physicality, in all his vigour, races in to fill me up. His lips are stained with dark wine. He rubs his cheek with the palm of his hand as if shy. He's examining the tapestry, peering at the lynx with her bloody beard and yellow eyes. Without a word, he grins at me and steps backwards as if he's readying to leave, and I find I am running to get to the door before him, which I do and slam it shut, pressing my back to it.

So close to me now, he lowers himself to his knees, his hand slipping beneath the hem of my inner tunic. Almost too quickly, he has removed my shoe and is picking up my foot. The sensation of his skin on mine, his thumb rubbing my heel, his index finger drawing a line from my ankle, down, down to my little toe. Now his fingers are climbing ever so slowly up my calf. His hand reaches my knee, circles it, gently stroking the flesh nestled where my leg bends. My breath is heavy as his fingers let go and climb higher. I grip his shoulders, and I am lowering, already damp for him, but someone is knocking on the door, and his hand has let me go. He is standing, guiding me to one side. He is opening the door, and I am hit with the sound of women's voices yelling.

He steps into the passage, and I fumble to get my shoe on, before giving up and rushing out into a clamour of girlish bodies. I follow them out into the street. A family of girls all dressed in bright mantles is piling into a horse-drawn cart. Adam climbs up beside his pale-faced wife and, grinning, waves to me. I watch as he puts his arm around her shoulders, strokes the obtrusion of her belly and whispers in her ear. She laughs. She hasn't seen me, but I watch her as the cart rolls down the street.

❧ The Workroom ❧

Come here to me, all you in need of coin. I am ready and waiting, here alone. Find me in a stone cell. The laughter has not yet died, but there is no sky overhead, only the planks hewn from trees that once grew in a forest.

Come. I am here alone, the walls stuffed so full of metal coins all sound from the city beyond has been cut off. Here it is cold in the winter and hot in the summer. The chairs are hard, despite the cushions. There is ash at the bottom of the brazier, and the lamps cast smoke to hang around the heads of anyone who enters.

Here, it is easy to forget the road taken to arrive. There is no one to talk to. No one to take your hand and delve into the shadows with you.

🌿 A Report from Callan 🌿

"He's all alone now with four daughters."

"What a nightmare."

"So many women."

"Who's dead?"

"Ah, Mistress Outlaw, you startled me."

"Tell me who's dead."

"What'll you pay us for the knowledge?"

". . . Thank you, kindly. It's Dametta. Wife of le Blund."

"It was the baby that killed her dead."

"Tore her up."

"Ripped her open."

"And the baby?"

"Dead too."

"Hah, the Kyteler woman left quick."

"Give me my coin."

"Kyteler wants more babes, don't you think?"

"At her age? That one is touching forty."

"Aye. Kyteler's all withered inside."

❧ July 1301 ❧

No matter if I reach for the sky, attempting Heaven, this town holds me in its filth. I am standing in front of a fine house in Callan. I have fled my smoky workroom. All day, I rode hard, two armed servants galloping wildly behind me. Now, I smell of horseshit and horse sweat. I reach into my drawstring purse at my waist and pull out my stoppered bottle of perfume, dabbing it on my forehead and rubbing it on my teeth. It stings my tongue with a dusty, fruity flavour. I have come for Adam. My need for him tastes vicious and desperate. I am afraid as I pass through the unbolted door, up the stairs and into the best room. I am afraid as I find him sitting on the edge of the bed, pulling on his wool inner tunic. He looks up at me, startled mouth opening. He doesn't move towards me, but now he's leaping, his arms opening wide, encircling me in warmth and the smell of sandalwood and sweat.

"You're widowed," I say.

"Am I?" His hair looks like the hackles of a dog. He laughs, pressing his nose against my forehead.

"I rode all day to be with you," I say.

The blanket on his bed moves as if possessed by a ghost, and the white-capped head of a woman appears. She rubs her eyes.

"Your servant," I say.

He nods, grinning. "Kyteler, you disturbed a man in bed."

"I'll be waiting downstairs."

❧

The walls of the hall are hung with tapestries. The largest is stitched onto plain linen and depicts a summer garden of flowers. It must be her handiwork. Dametta. The pale threads will soon fade almost to white, and, at a distance, it will be impossible to tell one bloom from the other. I step out into the courtyard and demand wine from a servant. Back in the hall, I warm myself by the large fire at the centre of the room. On every bench there are bright cushions. He must've chosen them, for the dead wife's taste, I am sure, was bland.

A girl of about fifteen steps into the room, her arms crossed tightly over her chest. Her lips are white and drawn in a harsh line, a scar where her mouth ought to be. Like her mother, her forehead is fashionably high and pink from plucking. As is the style of the moment, she has no eyebrows at all. I have not bothered with this yet. My eyebrows have always been pale, and I have seen enough bodily alterations come and go in my forty years to know it's not worth it if in a few years I have to regrow hair which may refuse to come back.

"I am sorry for the loss of your mother," I say.

"Are you really?" The skin around her eyes is puffy and grey.

"No," I say, "I suppose I'm not particularly sorry. You see I never knew her, but I assume it is a great loss to you and your sisters. For that I am sorry."

"It was a loss to my father too!"

"I'm sure."

"She was everything a wife and mother ought to be."

"And what is that?"

"Selfless and God-fearing," she says with the thrust of someone older, someone who is male. I can't help but like her for this confidence.

"Like you, I assume," I say.

She shakes her head. "No. No, I am not like her. I am always angry with my husband. I am not at all what I ought to be."

"At least you're honest," I say. "But people will take advantage if you always reveal yourself. Tell me, are all your sisters married?"

She scowls at me, her eyes roaming my face, assessing my danger. I am a threat to all young women for I am a rich widow. A better catch than any girl.

"The youngest isn't," she says. "She's only twelve."

Adam appears beside her and pats her arm, but she shakes him off.

"You've met Alice Kyteler then," he says.

"Don't be a fool, Father," she says. "She's Outlaw."

She marches out of the room, but I sense she must be hovering in the hall.

"Well." He cocks his head to one side, grinning.

"Shall we marry?" I say.

He laughs. "Christ in Heaven, you're beautiful."

I approach the largest tapestry and pull at the loose thread of a bluebell, a symbol of beauty, a carrier of grief. I tug hard at the thread until only the small needle pricks are visible in the fabric, the thread balled in my fist. I turn back to him and find he is kneeling on the floor.

"Don't speak to me in the words of other men," I say.

"This is what they do, isn't it?" he says. "Men beg and grovel and simper and weep." He leaps to his feet. "I will demand. You will be my wife."

"I have come all this way," I say. "You will have to do better."

He laughs, deeply from his belly, collapses to his knees again and falls slowly backwards onto the floor. He watches, blue eyes sparking with light, as I shut the door.

I stand above him, shake my foot from my shoe and press it to his chest. Slowly, he's reaching for my bare skin, but there's a rapping at the door. He leaps up and yanks it open.

"Yes?" he growls.

But it's no one. Just a servant bringing the wine, which he grabs from her, shutting the door in her face. He turns to me, beaming.

"I must admit," he says, "I am all spent this morning. I can give you pleasure but not myself."

I slot my hands behind my back, push out my chest. "We have the rest of our lives."

He bounces up to me and retrieves both my hands from behind my back. "My lightning woman."

My heart is battering against my ribs. He lifts my hands to his neck. He must feel me shaking. I am in his power now, but all the same, I tell him, "You will do as I say."

"With pleasure."

LE BLUND

❧ July 1301 ❧

It's near sunset. Sheep drink from a stream, dog roses wave in the breeze, and, ahead, the forest, lush and green, is calling to me. I tell the servants to go on with the cart and unload it at my inn. I turn my horse towards the trees, and, oddly obedient, my new husband follows me. Soon the watchmen will close Kilkenny's gates, locking us out, but I don't care if we have to spend the night under the stars. We will warm each other.

I slip down from my mare, tie her reins to a branch and, without looking back, run into the forest. I leap over ferns and tree roots, dart around bushes and stones. I hear him trampling behind me and spin and leap into his arms. I've caught him. Finally. We collapse onto the moss-dense ground. On my tongue, his salt sweat, and in my nose, the dense smell of forest soil. Swiftly, he is inside me, and almost immediately, I shatter the air with my cries, sending birds screeching from their branches. He roars and flops back against the ground, eyes shut. With such ease, I felled him. I gaze up at the forest roof. Between the leaves I see snatches of sky burning. Sunset.

Beneath me, he is smiling, rubbing his eyes, as if he might fall asleep, tempting me to nestle against him and drift into dreams, safe in his clutches. But I am not ready for rest. I want more.

"Wife," he says, "I am not made of wood. I need to recover before I can start again."

I climb off him, my skin tingling still, and take a few strides away from him. Between the trees, in the distance, I can make out Kilkenny's grey walls.

"You're fierce," he says. "If I didn't know already, I would say you've never fucked before. What was Outlaw at?"

"Very little," I say, still staring at the city.

"What a fool. You were wasted on him."

"Make me a promise," I say, striding back to him.

His hands are propped behind his head, a lazy expression on his mouth.

"Promise this won't change between us," I say. "Promise you'll be loyal to me no matter what."

"Are you suspicious of my fidelity, little cat?" He reaches for my ankle, but I step just out of his reach.

"I don't care what you do outside my bed," I say, "but you must be obedient to me and my son, to our house. Above your own."

He pushes himself to sitting, his gaze stern.

"Swear," I say.

He fists the ground and jolts himself to standing.

"I swear it, little wife." He reaches for me, but I step away.

"On the lives of your daughters," I say.

"I am yours now." He grasps my mantle in his fist. "And you are mine."

I snatch my mantle away from him. "Swear on your girls."

Frowning, he fixes his gaze on me. "God strike you, Alice. The girls are all wed but one. We've left the others to feed her till she's old enough. You have nothing to fear from them. I am yours."

"And Will."

"Sure. Throw in your son. Now may I have my reward?"

I kiss him full on the mouth. He bites my lip. He is angry, but this is the spark in him that I hungered for. This is the man I wanted.

In the fading light, we ride through Kilkenny's gates. Impaled above it, the heads of thieves and killers are putrefying. My mouth is washed with the sharp taste of blood.

❧ Word from Callan to Kilkenny ❧

"Outlaw wasn't even cold."

"Le Blund. He's next, all right."

"But he was in on it."

"It was just her. Only a woman could."

"The court will hear it and give us the truth."

❧ May 1302 ❧

"We're accused of murder."

Adam sits with his chair pulled right up to Roger's table, his knees bouncing. The room is layered with blankets and cushions, the floor insulated by many overlapping rugs as bright as summer meadows. Vastly impractical for eating. Perhaps a man like Roger, a Templar with influence, can afford to replace his rugs each spring, after the winter's trampling of food scraps. I could afford it too if I wanted, but despite my wealth I still have sense to put down rushes if I have a meal on the table.

"You must be calm," Roger says to Adam.

"I can't be calm," my husband says.

"I never ask him to be calm," I say.

"Would you be calm if you were me?" Adam says.

Roger puts down his pen. "I need this resolved."

"I barely knew your brother," Adam says. "How could I have killed him? Sure, I was in town that night, but I certainly wasn't at Alice's inn. I'd never have gone into her bedchamber. There was nothing between us before. Nothing we acted on anyway. We'd met, sure, but I never touched his property. Look, I'm shaking."

Roger's wife, pink-cheeked and young, stands against the panelling like an ornament, pretending deafness, but I can tell from her intent, dark eyes she is drinking in every word. I ought to befriend her, take her into my workroom sanctuary, feed her cakes and make her share all she's heard in this room, but, still, after so many years, I find I cannot like the wife of Roger.

His brown eyes dart over me. I gaze back at him, focused on steadying my breath. I am sure he still trusts me. I would read it in those large, dark eyes if he thought I had betrayed him.

Adam picks up a half-eaten pie from a plate and takes a massive bite. "Murdering. Us!" He sprays crumbs across Roger's rugs.

"William would hate this," Roger says, rubbing the bridge of his nose. "He wouldn't bear the shame of his name, his wife's name or his son's being tarnished like this."

"None of my people have discovered who has accused us," I say.

"But you suspect someone." Roger straightens in his chair. "Tell me."

All of Adam's daughters beg him for coin, for advice, for whole days out of his week. They tell him all I wanted was his fortune, and he replies with his laugh, saying, "She's only human." These daughters slink away, trying to avoid me, but I stand in the hallway waiting, smiling, telling them they look well, and most of them are ashamed enough to blush.

"My stepdaughters," I say.

Adam drops the pie, and it splinters apart. "They'd never."

I kneel on the floor beside him. "Think, my love. They despise me. And if we're found guilty, they'd inherit everything. This alone is enough to inspire them. They'd do all they could to take our poor Will's inheritance too. You must change your testament. Write them out."

"No—"

"They're intent on seeing me, and you, my love, hung."

"Whoever it is has no case." Roger stands up. "We know my brother was old and passed in his sleep. The surgeon confirmed it. I will get him to speak on your behalf."

"I will pay whatever sum is required," I say, "but no more."

"Understood."

Adam slaps the table, shattering the pie further. "We're innocent. We shouldn't spend a penny."

"That's never been how the law works, le Blund," Roger says.

Adam puts his head in his hands. He is crying, and I am too shocked to move to comfort him. It's Roger's wife who pats his shoulders and tells him everything will be well, that her husband can solve anything. She leads Adam out of the room with the promise of good beer.

"We need never go to court at all," I say, pacing, eyes on the floor. "Bribing a jury will prove expensive, so we send witnesses to the sheriff. They will state they saw Adam drinking until late at his inn, and more from my household will vouch for me. The sheriff is easily bought, but it can't come through me. You must speak to him. Be candid, as he responds well to that, but covert too, just in case."

"Alice?"

"I can only guess it was one of the daughters, and if that is true, the case will be thrown out, for how could any of them be witnesses? They were all in Callan when William died."

"Alice!"

"What?"

"Am I right?"

I stop. "About what?"

For a moment, he doesn't respond. He's staring at the piece of pie Adam has mutilated.

Finally, he meets my gaze. "Were you the one who sent this accusation to the sheriff?"

I sink onto the settle. "What gave me away?"

Roger laughs, but it's a cold, sad laugh. "You want Adam to write his daughters out of his testament."

Now, I laugh, but the sound is too bright. "You found me out."

"You never could keep a secret from me," he says.

In silence we both enter shadow memories. I am only pulled back from them by Roger's hand grasping mine.

"Consider the charges dropped and his wealth all Will's."

I squeeze his fingers. "You're a true friend."

"Don't I know it. You're likely to be the end of me."

* * *

The tops of trees shiver and a white shaft of light falls to the grass. Beyond me, in the forest's depths, there is no sound except the cuckoo calling me. She is the bringer of love and summer. She is the bird of deception and adultery. She fools others into raising her children. She is quick and clever. She is telling me to go home, to wake up.

I wake knowing I have escaped with my life. The trap I set myself proved more tricky to wriggle out of than I had anticipated, but Roger, as I had gambled, came through. His word with the sheriff was all I needed. The case was dismissed, at little cost to me, and the whisperers soon will move on to other scandals. Adam now fears his daughters and has banned them all from visiting—the youngest too, who even I can't claim could have reported us—yet, still, I know he hasn't sent for a clerk to change his testament. He drinks more, and sometimes, in the evening, after too much wine and listening to a traveller's tale, tears well in his angry eyes. He feels bitter at his daughters, but also, I fear, I sense, even more bitter with me.

"Adam?"

He dozes beside me, his eyelashes sweetly fluttering.

"Adam."

"Mmm."

"You cannot let them inherit."

"Alice," he groans, "it's too early."

"We escaped with our lives, but all could turn against us next

time. Everything, all your coin and property, must go to Will . . .
and me."

"Whatever you say."

I reach inside his tunic and find him soft, but he feels my presence. He growls. I laugh and climb on top of him.

❧ Places I Have Fornicated with My Husband ❧

* Just before dawn on my workroom floor with the door wide open.

* By daylight, against the garden wall, half concealed by an apple tree: swift, but pleasurable.

* In the back of a cart beneath the open sky on the way to Callan. We paid the driver off, but he still mentioned it in the tavern afterwards, and word reached Kilkenny a week later.

* In St. Mary's churchyard, not long after curfew, when a night-watchman might catch us: a great sin, and so all the more thrilling.

* Twice in a guest room with guests: a beautiful couple, especially her; and an excessively energetic monk who was far too young for us.

* In every place mentioned we take the positions the priests tell us are the most sinful, with me, the woman, on top or, almost as profane, like animals with him entering me from behind.

❧ May 1303 ❧

I am a house full of emotions, but there is nothing new in my extremes. One moment I am joy, the next full of despair, and by evening I am in a listless ease. I am never still, never occupying one sensation, usually all feelings all at once and sometimes none at all. It is all because of Adam. At night, we meet in the dark, hands reaching. My skin has always been firm, never bruised easily, but now come wash day I am marked with fresh green fingerprints and old grey marks. We stain my skin with our ferocity, but I hardly care, despite the aches.

In daylight, when we are not bodies but minds at work, we gather coin, and oh how well we amass it; we are like two dragons ready to breathe fire on anyone who might try to take it from us. Sometimes, I catch him staring at me with the hunger of the wolf, and I know my answering expression is a mirror.

Now, we are in the workroom, me at my table going over the morning's takings, him laying back on the settle, swilling a cup of beer.

"Let's promise now," he says, "to die only when we're ancient, in the same instant, side by side in our bed."

"I plan never to die," I say, "but I shall hold your hand as you do."

He leaps up, his beer splashing on my rug. He gulps the rest and throws the cup on the settle where it lands on a cushion. He runs around my table, grabs my wrists and pulls me to standing, our bodies now pressed against each other. His tongue travels to my ear. I shudder. The door is shut but not bolted. Any guest or servant might enter, and this makes me want him more. He presses his hand against the soft place where my legs meet, and I am glad I am wearing only a thin silk cyclas. He strokes me, and quick, almost too quickly, I am trembling, I am gasping. He pushes me so I am knelt behind the table on the floor. I lift his tunic, untie his breeches and find him hard. I tease him with my tongue, but he curses, and so I get to work. Too soon, I am spitting his seed on the floor for a servant to deal with later. He is soft and supple now where once he was solid and rough. Already, I long for more. The tingling on my skin reaches inside me, carving out spaces between my bones. I press my mouth to his, and he groans softly. I lift my own tunic, show him myself, and he laughs, and while he watches I touch myself. My body is humming, and I am gasping, shaking harder than before. At the peak, I cry out and like a wild thing let my hand fall from myself, leap on him and bite. He holds me, stroking my hair, and guides me to the settle, where we both collapse, no doubt breaking his ceramic beer cup.

"Sometimes I wish to go to Hell," I say.

He rubs his lips against my ear. "I would join you."

"To me Heaven seems such a clean and boring place."

He sighs, his eyes fixed on the rafters where I have hung meadowsweet to keep the room fresh.

"Hell," I say, "is similar to how we live now on earth. It's dirty and messy and full of pain, but there is so much pleasure too. What jokes could we share in Heaven?"

"I know a clean joke."

"Do tell."

His forehead wrinkles, and he rubs his cheek with an open palm.

"What did the serpent say to Eve when they met at the tavern after the Fall?"

"I can see where this is going."

"I bet you can. Let me introduce you to him again."

❧ March 1305 ❧

Kilkenny's nobles are all ravenous, licking their teeth and sniffing the cathedral's air for the thrill of perfume. It is the day before the end of Lent. Everyone is planning their first meat meals. I have ordered four honey-glazed piglets and a flock of pheasants.

Adam's fingers creep across my thigh, and I slap his hand away. Here it is too much. I have some reputation to keep. According to our priests: once a week ought to be sufficient; never when a woman bleeds (but as my bleedings have become erratic I sin less often in this way); it goes without saying that adultery is a grave sin (yet the priests mention it almost every Sunday); and fornication during Lent will cost a deal of prayers and a bag of coins to absolve. I doubt half the knights sat beneath St. Canice's soaring roof have followed these rules; I certainly have ignored them, but still the place sparks with a furious hunger, which tells me there's been a deal of denial.

The bishop wriggles in his baggy silk alb like a stoat in a trap who knows he shall soon be made into a furry purse.

"Bodily pleasure," he says, his voice coming at us from odd angles, "it is but for a moment. The fire which follows thereon you will endure for ever."

He is thinking about the boy who lives with him, eating sweet fruits from his hands and, in return, whipping the naked Bishop of

Ossory. He is thinking about the cold coin he now owes me for my knowledge. He is thinking how he can squirm out from under my thumb. But I have even better than him. Last month, I trapped England's greediest wolf. King Edward owes me £500. The knowledge has made Adam and me as giddy as children.

"You cat," Adam whispers now.

He smells like eel pie and straw and burning animal fat. Softly, he growls. He's still hooked to the dawn. I woke with a weight on my chest. Since his daughters' accusation—or, to be accurate, mine—he has become rough with me, sometimes pushing his way inside me before I am made ready, twice making me bleed, and sometimes, ignoring my cries of pain, feigning he believes they come in pleasure, and always this begins while I am still sleeping. He would never dare start in this brutal fashion if I was vivid, awake and glaring into his eyes. This morning, I woke and found him pressing down on me. Before I could demand he get off, the door of the bedchamber burst open. It was just a servant girl. She gasped, giggled and scuttled out of the room, but I called her back to dress me. I wriggled out from under him and left him hard and irritated. Now, his hand snakes up my back. I slap it away.

In the pew in front of me, I watch the grey head of Richard de Valle. He is an anomaly. I don't know why he's here in Kilkenny, away from his rich pastures, his children. Perhaps he is running from his dead wife. All of us who live long enough have our shades. Yet he is still calm, despite his loss. He is a stillness I would like to sink into.

A finger touches the back of my neck. Adam, but, no, he is leaning towards Will, whispering in my son's ear. I turn and am met by the smug gaze of John le Poer. He must've slipped in to sit behind us just before Mass began. He leans back against the pew, the lines of him flowing with threat. He has pale, hairless hands; in his lap, they look slippery. He rubs his lip with the finger that must have stroked my neck. He's smiling. For a man in his late forties, he is more handsome than when I first met him, and, just like then, I long to flee, but also I long to grab his arm before I go and take him with me. We stay staring at each other until the bishop is silent and Adam grasps my hand in his. I don't shake him off. I turn back to him. He is forgiven for this morning. He is forgiven for thinking he is my master. I whisper, loudly, in his ear what we will do tonight.

❧ A Coloured Manuscript Illumination ❧

Price: unknown

A man and his wife on a garden path, close to a river. All around them are wild poppies and brilliant blue cornflowers. His rich clothing suggests he is a Templar, a banker or even a Deputy Justiciar or Chancellor of Ireland. She is dressed simpler, yet in the way he leans on her, it is clear she is the one he goes to for advice, forgetting his fellow men, and even his childhood friends, those who know him better than anyone.

The couple are clearly easy with each other. They appear almost to be a single being, heads bent close, perhaps gently laughing or weeping, but most definitely sharing all that is inside them, their souls. They are the picture of felicity and trust.

But disturbing the perfect tableau, at the bottom of the illumination, the wimpled head of a rich woman intrudes, watching.

❧ September 1306 ❧

Our bedchamber door is half open. On the side table, a bowl of lilies lies abandoned, caught in a shaft of light. I tear off my silk headscarf. I wore it for Adam, but I haven't seen him all day. I so rarely need him in the day, but this day, I do. I have a need to walk in the garden or, no, the meadow and tell him about my childhood which I so rarely visit, even in my own mind, and when I tell him, once all the words are out, we will run into the forest. We will hold each other, naked, beneath red and gold leaves. We will rest in each other's arms, becoming one, at peace.

It cannot be long before he appears. I've sent two servants out to search for him. I am almost breathless in my waiting. Turning, I find I am no longer alone in the bedchamber. A tomcat stands on the rug, spitting. His head is massive, too large for his muscled body, and his bottom lip is swollen from a fight. I slam my feet on the floor, but he doesn't run. He is in search of a fish head or a heated female who he can shove his barbed spike inside. I jump onto the bed. My legs are bare. I wear only my under-tunic. A scratch from him could turn vile, weep pus and kill me. I cannot risk his claws. This cat is not worth my life.

He prowls the entire room, sniffing, and crawls beneath the bed, searching. It is my bleeding. I have drawn him to me with my smell of coins rubbed together.

I wait for him to reappear, to leave. I wait until the bones in my legs ache. I can't call for a servant because a guest might enter the bedchamber and see me undressed. I hold myself rigid, waiting for him to bore of me, to find a meatier victim. I watch as he slips out from under the bed, but, instead of prancing out, he just continues his pacing. He is all muscle, mantled in brilliant flaming fur. Back and forth, back and forth he goes, never once stopping to sit and lick his wounds. I am ready, on all fours. I will fight him if I must. He approaches the bed. My mouth is loaded. I spit. It hits his massive face, and he leaps back, streaking from my bedchamber.

I whoop and throw the door closed, run to my wooden chest and take out my clothes to air for tomorrow. I focus on keeping my hands firm, deliberate. I focus on each fabric as I shake it out. Linen. Silk. Wool. I laugh. A cat. It was just a cat, but my heart is still pounding. I am still afraid. I fold each cyclas and tunic and place them back inside the chest.

❧

I have been awake all night, pacing the lamplit bedchamber. My breast is numb, but my feet feel quick with energy. I resist their urge to run. Adam, head bare, is poking my lilies floating in their bowl. He turns towards me, his fist clenched, his eyes bright with tears, and it comes to me like a flash. He knows what I did in the dark of this room. Perhaps he sensed it each night in my sharp nails and teeth. Perhaps that's why he hurt me. But, no, he couldn't know before. Someone has told him.

He lifts his hand from the bowl, fingers dripping. All the nights he spent up late drinking with Will. I joined them in the evenings, but then they moved to the taverns or on to watch a cock fight. I was too fond of sleep. I wouldn't sully my reputation by joining them. But Will would never spill my secret for any reason, except perhaps the love of a father.

I hear a ringing, but the bells can't yet be calling. If only I could run to the cathedral and get the ringers to unring the bells, to take us back to yesterday. I give him my smile-smirk. He is red. Red hair, red mouth, red heart. I long to take his old heart, the one from yesterday, to cut it out and keep it for ever in the chest at the end of my bed, for then we would be preserved as we were, him in blissful ignorance and I with a husband mostly tamed.

I step towards him, but he pushes past me, bends over my wooden chest and yanks out tunic after tunic, tossing them behind him like he's disembowelling a carcass. I stumble towards him, push my tunics back inside, but he continues hurling them—yellow, red, blue.

"Hah," he cries and darts forward.

His fist is clenched, and I leap at it, try to wrench it open.

"That was my mother's."

He pushes me to the floor. The door shrieks. The inn is too silent, but it is night. It is always silent at night.

"I only ever drank it myself," I call.

I find I am chasing after him. I find we are at the top of the stairs, grappling, and then I find I am no longer grappling. I am still and I am alone, and in my hand I hold my mother's vial of poison.

He is still too. He lies at the bottom of the stairs, arms wide, palms up. His mouth is open. His sky-blue tunic is stained. It is dawn. The only reason I can see him is because the door to the street is wide, and I don't know if he left it open on his way up or a wayward guest or servant has just come in. I listen for footsteps or voices but hear nothing except my own panting.

Slowly, I descend the stairs. I step over him and walk out onto the street, leaving the door open behind me.

Once, the nettle was a beautiful flower in the Garden of Eden, but after Eve tempted Adam the serpent hid beneath it, and the green leaves began to sting anyone who touched them.

"Are you all right?" De Valle stands in the empty doorway of a ruined church. He has an undyed wool hood pulled over his head to protect him from the soft rain falling through the empty roof.

"It's not May," I say, turning back to the stinging leaves. "It's too late to gather nettles. The Devil is out to get them for his tunic."

"The blood." He's pointing at my feet. I am still in my house shoes, soft and lined with rabbit fur. Adam's blood has soaked into them.

Adam. I have lost his skin, the salt taste of his shoulders, the daily prickle of his beard against my neck, the wrinkles that shot out from his eyes when he laughed. I have lost bodily pleasure. I have lost laughter, his and mine. I will never again hear the noisy force of his jibes or the boom of his shout for wine or bread or me. Lost is the thrill of our fighting. Lost is the man I could tell that the God we hear about from the pulpit was created to line the purses of greedy men. No one else will laugh at such unholy words. No one else knows everything worth living for is unlawful.

"I didn't hold his hand," I say, "I meant to. I really did."

De Valle is close to me now. His fingers cold against my forehead.

"You're unseasonably warm," he says.

"Pull up a nettle," I tell him, "say my name, and I will be cured."

"I will take you home, if you'll allow me."

I reach out for the nettles, take leaves in my hand. The heat shoots up my arm and into my head.

"I don't know what happened," I say.

"I've been told he fell. The word has already spread across the city. My servants said you were known to have run off in your grief and no one could find you, but I thought you might have come beyond the walls, out here where it's greener. I prefer it myself. This church is where I retreat. It seems to me where God can be his truest self."

I am standing on a tombstone. It's on tombstones and dead places where nettles grow. The abandoned and uninhabited places. Nettles are ghosts.

"This blood isn't yours," he says.

"It's all mine. All his blood is mine."

I didn't mean to push him. It was my bleeding. It took over my hands, made them hard with rage, and it was dark. He just fell. It was the stone slabs at the bottom of the stairs that killed me. Not me. Him. They made so much blood. I have never seen so much blood.

I long to rest, to put my head against the softness of de Valle's wool hood and sink into another life, but I don't. I gather my bundle of nettles, hold them to my chest, feel them tickle and sting my face. I am going back to the inn where the goose will be laid out on the dining-room table ready for a meal, and laid out on my workroom table will be my love.

"I will walk back beside you," de Valle says.

I don't have the strength to push him away. I don't want to push him away.

❧ August 1307 ❧

"I'm glad I found you," de Valle says.

I am bent over in the garden, using my shears to cut lavender in the rain. The flowers have burst between the sprouting branches of the willow fence. Leeks, onions and kale all grow too close together. The borders are full of sorrel and mint, and there are daisies everywhere to attract the bees and dragonflies.

I had fallen asleep on my workroom settle and woken up, cold and shaking, and so I came out to the garden to prowl. Adam used to walk through my thoughts, always softly weeping, never truly the man I adored, instead a shadow, always just out of my reach, but now, a year later, it's worse. He has stopped entering my mind with any clarity at all, and I am left searching for his scent, the specificity of how his mouth curled to laugh, but I smell nothing, see nothing. Adam is the power and the base of my being. He is deep inside me, for ever. To rid my soul of him would be to kill my soul, yet still he has faded, and so I too am fading.

We're at the water's edge, de Valle and I. The rain is heavy. No servant will venture into the garden now, but they might well stand at the door and look out. I am echoey. I long to rest my head on his shoulder, to shut my eyes and be peaceful. I long for what I can't have.

I long too for Will. It has gradually turned bitter between us. Since Adam's death we have been wary. I know he blames me, just as I blame him for revealing to my love what happened to my first husband. When he is near me we might as well be distant. We speak only of what's meaningless: the roads, the rain, the latest bishop. We never speak of what we fear.

Now beside me is a different man, and he doesn't know me. Still, he has tasted some of the strangest, saddest part of me, and he remains. Yet I am more than just the loss of Adam, or perhaps all I was before has fled. This last year, de Valle has visited me often, whenever he's passing through for business—and, I suppose, pleasure too. He brings strange gifts: cuttings from his own garden, manuscripts of poetry and astronomy he thinks might intrigue me. He is a rare bird of a man. Others bring me jewels and fabrics and horses. But he brings a pot of mint and a simple engraving of a verse about an English forest.

"May I?" He's holding out his hand. I nod, and his fingers lightly touch my back, his arm enclosing me, making this a place where I am innocent and blessed.

He seems sometimes like all the others. Drawn in by my faces: my come hither face; my love me face; my I want you face; my I am wealthy face; my I am so foolish face; my laughing face; my witty face; my utter despair. Yet, he is staring at me with such kindness. He never asks anything of me, only admires the plants, points out the ducklings floating after their mother on the river.

He's not handsome. His skin is blotched with red. There are creases around his mouth from smiling. He is a crease. He creases into a half-century. I know the angels are coming for him. They have already received the message and are airborne.

Daily, I must remind myself that it's Will's turn to marry now. He must find wealth in the arms of another. He must continue the line. But it won't be my name his children carry. It will be Outlaw's.

De Valle is a good name, but not mine.

De Valle asks me to take a walk; we'll bring servants and leave the city for the meadow.

"Yes," I say. "Why not?"

❧ Nuptials ❧

"She's done it again."

"Done what?"

"Married another."

"Who?"

"The Kyteler woman."

"Nobility now. Mighty ambitious, that woman."

"I always thought there was something unnatural about her."

"Jealous men all at the ceremony, watching."

"John le Poer chief. He was sure making eyes at the lady."

"And her brother-in-law? I always thought there was something between them."

"He was more taken with his dog than the lady."

"You mean his wife?"

"Well, yes, he does seem to care for his wife, but, no, he was prattling away to a puppy in his arms."

"The rich are so odd."

DE VALLE

❧ September 1310 ❧

I sit on the altar of the abandoned church and wait for my husband. He has been away in Tipperary to see his children, all grown, and all angry about his marrying me, the innkeeper and lender. He had asked me to come with him, but I refused. I have had enough of stepchildren. Instead, I told Richard to meet me here on the day of his return.

He enters, blinking against the sunlight streaming through the empty roof.

"Alice." Those eyes of his cast about as if looking for another word. He is offended at my sitting on God's table. His sweetness is enough to drive even the most placid saint into the wildest rage, and yet I care for him.

I jump down, go to him, press my face against his chest.

"I missed you," I say and enclose him in my arms.

"Why are we out here?" he says.

I kiss him, and he leans in, wrapping his mantle about me.

"I thought we might make love out here," I say.

"Not in God's house," he says. "Even if He has abandoned it."

I step backwards, but his cloak still hangs around me.

"We are always watched, aren't we?" I say.

"You more than me." He strokes my cheek.

He means my ghost, le Poer, whose wife finally died this year.

Not labouring for a child, but at the end of her labours. Age took her. It is the blessed way to depart the world, the turning in the path we all wish to reach, but her passing has given le Poer's stares a new urgency; yet I am sure he visits brothels nightly and feasts on more flesh than anyone could want. Perhaps he is more than sated by widowhood. Perhaps I merely imagine his obsession. I convince myself, but then I find him sat amidst my guests, laughing, and he will stop, mouth still half open, and stare at me with a familiar wolfish hunger. I imagine nothing. Still, he knows my power, because he rarely approaches me with more than a few words of greeting. I feel he is biding his days, waiting for the moment I will be found in weakness and invite him into my bed. I fear that day, because I too sense it.

"We could leave here," Richard says.

I see us wandering through London's markets, our hands clasped. I see us sat beside a river in Flanders, the birthplace of my father, and in the distance the forest is dark and creaking. It is true. I have never seen a seagull on the blue cloth of an ocean, nor the forests of Europe, but all are only imaginings. Faint reflections on the wall of dying fires. I see us return to the towns. I hear him coughing at night. I feel his strength ebb from his body as he presses himself to me. I smell his musty skin in death and watch him buried in ground unfamiliar to us. I watch myself standing alone in a foreign graveyard, no one there to hold me.

"My business," I say, "would collapse without me."

"Perhaps it is the moment to let Will take over?"

I swallow, and my throat burns with the effort.

Richard has been bringing Will and I back together. He saw the distance between mother and son, and quietly began his quest to mend us. At first he only brought Will into the inn on larger occasions, festivals and parties, but then during more intimate evenings with just Roger, his wife, Richard and me. These are relaxed occasions with shoes off, everyone close to the braziers, simple food and textured conversation. I begin to like Roger's wife, Joan, but better yet, Will and I begin to joke again. Still, a wound large enough will always scar. Some evenings, I hold myself apart from him, talking only to the others. On the next occasion I see him, he purposefully refuses to ask my advice about some new deal he's considering. We can never be what we were when he was a child. On long nights, I cling to Richard when I think of all I've lost.

"Our life is brief," he says. "Leave Will what you have built and let's go. My children are well cared for. We have this chance."

I step away from him, and his mantle falls from my shoulders.

"I worked all my life for what I have." I scratch the moss on the altar. "If we left, it would be just us. No one else."

"Yes." He is smiling. This is what he wants.

"But it would just be us," I say. "One day, just me."

Richard is quiet, watching me. I am the one to take his hand and slip back beneath his cloak again.

"What is it you love in me?" I ask.

"The way you talk so vastly of everything. How you know more about almost every subject than anyone in any room. The little dents that form in your cheeks when you are angry."

"But you don't really know me," I say.

"I know all I need to know."

And we do make love, but outside the church, in the long grass, watched only by birds in the branches of an oak tree.

After, nestled against his chest, I say, "I can't leave. Not yet."

He kisses my head.

"I know," he says. "I'll wait for you."

My beloved. He thinks everyone is as good as he.

❧ The Mouse ❧

I share my bedchamber with a small black mouse. It's like him, small and struggling to stay warm. I take pity on him, close him in my palm and carry him about. In the evening, I sit in the dining room telling marvellous stories for my guests about past encounters with men now famous and dead, and the mouse watches me, his eyes shining in the fire's glow. Those eyes. Even in the dark, they see. At night, the dead mute faces of saints on the tapestries listen to my moans of pleasure, my sweet husband against me, gently touching me the way I have come to like. By sunrise, the mouse is curled up in my lap, and we are all sweetness, but when a froth of my hair escapes my wimple, they look up, the mouse and my husband, and I'm sure they see me for who I truly am.

❧ September 1315 ❧

Outside, the river is becoming ice. It's slowing. Remembrances of the sun seep from my flesh and the nights are longer. I sink my hands into chests of coin, feeling out their brightness, but they are cool and slippery to the touch.

I cling to Will, trying to reanimate that free and easy way we once had with each other, but I know he longs to shake me off. He knows too much of me; my guilt wraps about him too. I am incapable of keeping anything from him. At least, he knows all I do about making coin. Now, he brokers as many deals as I, and I'm jealous. I am covetous of all contacts, even my son's. What a wicked mother I am to want to steal from my own child, but there it is.

Marry, I tell Will. She will bring you money, but he just laughs and says he has not yet met a woman who could please him for a lifetime.

I have no reply. My son is cleverer than me.

❧

Above the garden, swallows fly home. Richard walks slowly beside me, stooping, pointing out the plants that did well this summer and those which ought to be pulled up and put on the fire. He is grown frail these years. Last winter, the cold entered his chest and iced it over, and he's not yet thawed. I tell him to go back to his family, to his green, green lands, but he doesn't reply, only brings his lips to mine as if I am what gives him breath, and I think I want him to stay after all.

"Come." I take his hand, lead him inside the inn and up into my bedchamber.

"I have observed," I say, "that you often stare at the chest I keep so safely locked at the end of our bed."

"Yes." His voice is ever so soft now.

"Here." I undo the latch, and he reaches in without my telling, lifting out a slim roll of red silk.

"I will make you a hat from it," I say.

He shakes his head, smiling, stroking the fabric. His eyes are tender, laughing. They do so much of his talking for him now.

"You think it's not your colour, but red would suit you very well. You have a regal face."

He strokes my hand, still gazing into the chest, and shakes his head.

"Take out something else," I say.

He picks up the little bag that's sewn shut and holds it to his nose.

"Lavender," he says.

"Yes," I say.

"And?" he says.

"And my mother's fingernail clippings and hair. They were cut from her when she was dead. I kept them. It made me feel safer to have a part of her with me."

I lean in, stroke each item.

His eyes are on my face.

"My mother knew all about plants. Far more than me. I spent all my days studying my father's trade. I regret not learning from her. She was like you, I think. Quiet and thoughtful. I didn't value these qualities as a child."

His hand is on mine, holding me steady. I can't look at his face. I keep digging. He knows. I have never told Richard, but he senses the worst of my childhood. He knows I never left Will alone with any man when he was small. He knows I rarely mention my father, even though he is still a loved man in Kilkenny and many people mention him to me, but I always drive the conversation away from him, back to myself.

"This drink," I say, "it's made from foxglove. It cures colds and fevers. In this bottle is a tincture extracted from the yew leaf that will cause a slow, slow death. Strange, as the tree will live for thousands of years. This tea is for love. This ivy twig can be stirred in a drink, and it will dull a poison."

He straightens and lowers himself onto the bed.

"I will remember what you've said." He's smiling up at me. His face is so pale. I have worn him out. I try not to cry, but the tears come anyway.

❧ News Blows in from France ❧

"My grandfather's a witch. Always has been. If I told him he's now a heretic, he'd weep."

"Your grandfather's a gentle soul, but he'll have to change profession."

"Don't I know it."

"The Pope isn't really after your grandfather though. He wants bankers."

"I wish I could've seen those French usurers burn. Perhaps the same will be done here to our own coin swindlers."

"There's so much fat on them, they'd be sure to sizzle. The sparks would set Kilkenny alight."

"It will be Roger Outlaw who's burned first. He's a Templar. He's my bet."

"Ah, no. They won't go for him. He's over making Dublin safe from the Scots. Better that slippery woman of theirs."

"It'd be pleasing to hear a woman like her screaming."

"Shame her legs won't be open."

"Sure, haven't they been open long enough?"

❦ September 1316 ❦

"Wake up, Alice."

Richard's face is all lit up. He holds a lamp in one hand and coughs brutally into the other. His eyes are ringed in shadows, and he is so thin, almost wispy. He wraps his arms around me, strokes my back.

"I dreamed I was choking," I say. "A weight on my chest. I couldn't breathe."

He strokes my hair. "A cat jumped on you."

I laugh. "I know I shouldn't let them go everywhere, but I love them. Sometimes, they leave me gifts. Robins, tits, a lark, blackbirds."

"They think you cannot feed yourself."

He's gasping. Speaking is such a struggle for him now. I squeeze his hand until he's found his breath again. He smiles at me and strokes my cheek in thanks. He won't speak any more tonight.

"The cats leave the birds for you, Richard. I ordered the cook to make a few into pies. Only the freshest."

His eyes shine black in the light. I look into them. I have waited all these years for him to say he knows what I have done in the strange darkness of this room, that he knows who I was as a girl, half terrified, half adoring of her father, a girl turned bitter against men yet always in need of their devotion.

He pulls me to him, presses my head gently against his chest, so

I hear his heart, stuttering on. I squeeze him tighter than I should. I am trying to hold on to him. I am trying to stop him from leaving me.

*

With a corpse's smile, he whispers, "Do you hear the crickets chirping, my love?"

I press a kiss to his palm. "I will get a servant."

"Bring a lantern," he says. "It's dark."

He is fading. Every day he is fading. A man so kind can do nothing but fade. I feed him sweets ordered from the best vendor. Honey drizzled over dried fruits, but although he smiles and thanks me, he only pretends to eat them. Instead, when he has slumped asleep, I scoff what he has left hidden beneath his pillow.

For months, his bloodshot eyes beg me. He points to the chest. I refuse and refuse and refuse. I pretend I don't see what he wants, but he continues to gaze at me, and we both know I understand him completely. Eventually, he coughs, and there is too much blood. Later, once he is a pale creature in the bed, asleep, I stir water enhanced with yew needles, and when he wakes I give it to him to drink, to quicken his death. His eyes soften as he sips. I climb into the bed beside him and press my ear to his chest.

Everything good must die. That's why I keep living.

The True Tale of Margaret Russell

It's February in the year of our Lord 1311, five years before Richard de Valle will die in the bed of his wife. Alice is far from here, her head resting on the warm chest of her loving new husband. In sleep she is content and unknowing. But here in Mullinahone, there are twelve riders, black against the thinning snow. Above, the midday sun is lurid. On the edge of the valley ahead of them and shrouded on all sides by gentle Tipperary hills stands a stone farmhouse. Sheep sheltering beneath an oak tree scatter. The riders are merry on meat and beer. Their waists bristle with sheathed knives and swords. Their minds are dull from the long winter of inactivity. They are all chomping for a fight.

In front of the farmhouse, they clumsily rein in their horses and dismount, some tumbling from their saddles still drunk from the morning's beer. They slap their leader Stephen le Poer's shoulders as he swaggers on unsteady feet towards the door, but before he reaches it, he stops, and the men pause too like hunting dogs waiting for their master's release. All are still except a large-headed man with broad shoulders and feet planted wide apart. John le Poer, some twenty years senior to his cocksure nephew. Standing back with the horses, he watches, grey eyes a little bloodstained from lack of sleep and keeping up with the younger men, but still he smirks with the air of a man at a party.

A smile tears open Stephen le Poer's mouth, revealing sharp wet teeth. Like all the rest he is wrapped in a thick cloak, but unlike the others he has an ease in his loose-limbed body, announcing his confidence in his own righteousness. He turns to his men, and his bawdy laugh releases them. The hillsides ricochet eerily with the sound, but the men don't seem to notice the echo of their voices carried back to them from the past. They crowd around the door, joking with each other, some unsheathing their knives, although they know there is little need. No farmer has more than a few weapons, and they outnumber any quantity of people who overwinter on a farm.

The door leaps open. The farmer's wife has a wide forehead and large, dark eyes, reflecting fear. Looking up at the men, she seems to know her face must enrage and engorge them, but she has no power to change it.

"What do you want?" she says.

She holds her body stiff, trying to appear strong, but her shoulders shake. She wears a fine-spun but heavy wool tunic and a thick grey hood. Her lips are chapped from the cold. Flakes of her skin are caught around her collar. She stares at Stephen le Poer's left hand, which is extended to her.

"Margaret," he says, "my love. Come to me."

She takes a step back. He reaches through the doorway and grabs her about the waist, dragging her into the snow. He whirls her around in a dance, and the men whoop and cheer, and the sheep, not far off, tumble over each other towards the hills. Stephen spins her fast and, yelling with delight, lets go of her hands. Margaret tumbles backwards onto the ice-hardened snow. She sobs, but as the men form a ring around her she stops and presses her face into the snow: a begging stance. A vein pumps in Stephen's jaw. She stares at her naked red hands.

"What's the colour of your hair?"

"Look at the inside of her mouth. That'll show the colour of her clout."

"You said the girl was on fire for you."

"Dragged out here for a woman who's never seen him."

"Where's your husband, Marge?"

"We can't hear you."

"Stephen, she's a looker, but—"

"She's not looking at him—fuck, that hurt."

"Want to run away with me, Margaret?"

"Where's your husband?"

"The coward fled," she says, and they all laugh, and for this brief moment it seems as if she's won them over; glancing about, she laughs too as if she is one of them. This is the moment John le Poer steps into the circle. He wears the pleased expression of a man who's bet on a bear fight and has just seen that the opposition is malnourished and diseased. All the men, even his nephew, stare at him, and slowly he brings his hands together in prayer.

"My boy," he says, "you've brought us on a fool's journey to a married woman you said was in love with you, dying, you said, to be freed from the burden of her husband. Does she look to you like she's dying?"

"So what?" Stephen says. "So I saw her and liked the look of her."

John le Poer opens his hands wide. "We all have eyes, Stephen. We understand."

The men laugh, but Stephen, with the darting eyes of a rodent, senses the men are turning against him. He yanks Margaret up by her wrists and kisses her full on the mouth. Her body is stiff. He throws her aside. Blood trickles down his face. She has bitten him.

Without looking back, she starts running. She can hear the stamp of a horse's hooves behind her, but she keeps running until she falls and the breath is knocked out of her. She is filled with rage. She pushes herself back up, finds her feet and runs, but her breath is again stolen. She is yanked off her feet and dragged onto a horse. She bounces hard, her back ricocheting against a man's chest.

Everything ahead of her is hidden beneath snow. Behind her, she feels the hot and panting breath of the man, and she considers leaping off the horse, but she can hear the yells of the other men, delighted, raging for the chase. She clings on, but for what she holds on for, what future he has decided for her, she doesn't yet know.

She thinks, I'll miss my life, as lacking as it was, I'll miss it.

❧ June 1317 ❧

All the party guests are wearing animal masks. Wolves dance with rabbits, and horses tell mice their secrets, but I, a cat, am all alone. My owl, my Richard, is gone almost a year. The flocks of his children harangue me for money they claim is theirs, and I must send blunt letters of refusal. My grown cub, Will, is gone too. He is in Dublin with Roger. My pack have all left me.

I drink wine and more wine, dance with a goat, ask twice his name and laugh when he won't reveal it. His accent is lush, grown under a hot sun, I think, and made rusty by salty air. My mask covers only the top of my face. It is sewn with red fox fur and the tapered holes to see through are lined in black to accentuate the green of my eyes. As the night drifts on, the goat's human hands refill my copper goblet. Those hands lead me into the empty garden and down towards the water. There, I pull off my mask, reveal myself to him by the light of the hunter's moon, but he keeps his mask in place, and I don't ask him anything about himself, least of all if he will show me his face. A mysterious man from far away is just what I want tonight. We speak of fine food and rich clothes and desire. He asks me what my fantasies are, and I tell him. I tell him about the white flame inside me. I tell him how petals ought to be stroked gently. I tell him how sometimes I want to vanish, to lose so much breath I see the stars. He tells me I can see them now should I wish it, and I agree, but we don't move from under the rowan to gaze at the sky. I tell him it's dangerous to be alone with me. I tell him I once met a cat who killed a sheep. He laughs and tells me it's impossible, I must have dreamed it. I tell him dreams can be more real than waking. I long to press my lips to his. I tell him who I am by dark, what I have done. My mouth is telling him I gave poison to my owl, my love, and my mouth opens to tell him about Adam's blood and William's breath, but the Devil catches me at the waist, and I reach for his mask, lift up the goat and there beneath is the smirk I know so well. The Devil man. John le Poer. He bends and presses his smug lips to mine. His tongue jabs at the wall of my teeth. My mouth is pooling with liquid. All I taste is dread. I cannot squirm away. His hands are hard on my waist. I think about gold. Gold is the answer to all my questions. It clashes and it comforts.

I pull my lips from his and rest my head on his shoulder. The red moon is reflected in the river. Its flesh breaks apart on the black water, floating downstream towards the bridge. The night is brighter than many days I have lived through. I find it suddenly all too real. My fur ruff is scratching my skin. I think, I can do this with him. I have done worse.

"I have a proposal for you," le Poer says.

"Is it a proposal of marriage?"

"It is," he says, his hands still firm on my waist. "Tell me tomorrow when you've had a chance to think about what it would mean to say no."

"The answer is yes," I say, because he knows who I am now, what I have done, and if I don't give him myself, I am sure he will destroy me.

Those oiled lips curve slowly into a smile of delight. Some nights, with William or Adam, I imagined what it would be like to lie with le Poer. He was a kind of dream, but one I never really wanted in the waking day. Still, he is mine now. I place my hands on top of his, still grasping my hips, and remove them.

"Well," he says. "Well." His expression is euphoric. He thinks he is bending me to his will, and he almost did, but I am still in control. Many a wife or husband gives a tincture of yew to end their spouse's or even a child's suffering. He cannot judge me for it, nor can he think to report me to the sheriff. No, all I have done is make him want me more. All I have done is show I am a wife who cares. I am a wife worth having.

I examine him by moonlight. It's the best light to view one who will become a lover, and, even in the moon's red glimmer, he is handsome. He is what he claimed to be beneath the mask. The most devious of men—an angel who is damned—and I think, we are so alike, he and I.

"Kiss me again," he says.

I step away. "Not until we are wed."

He smirks. My refusal is a game to him.

"You and me," he says. "It was always going to happen."

The moon is vast and bright and bleeding.

LE POER

❧ July 1317 ❧

I watch the Devil weeping and I laugh.

On its wagon, the stage seems to float above the crowd. The Devil is the best of the actors, the best of the characters. He is loved for the way he springs onto his hands in delight and shakes his fists in fury. His mask is grotesque, but I have heard people talking; beneath it, they all believe he is more beautiful than any man they ever saw. Everyone shouts for the hero Theophile to be damned. After all, the fool sold his soul to the tricksy Devil. He sentenced himself already. Whipped up in the glee and splendour of the drama, the crowd cheer for his death, longing to see him burn. Yet, on his high stage, Theophile is living out all the people of Kilkenny's fantasies: youth and beauty, wealth and power. Few will ever reach the heights of those who have sold their souls. Yet to me the play is too simple. Half the churchmen I know have sold their souls to the Devil and bought back their right to purgatory with coin. Any rich man can save himself. It is the poor who can't afford to lose God's favour. Even I, banker that I am, can see the fallibility in this approach. When I reach death, I won't be one to bribe already rich men for Heaven. I will simply vanish and, with my wit and a heavy purse, attempt an end better than any a priest or bishop could offer me.

We were married on St. Swithin's Day, unsurprising now I come to think of it. Swithin was a spoilt bishop who, when his remains were not buried in the place he wanted, caused the sky to rain for forty days until his useless bones were moved. I saw the glint in my husband's eyes. He felt he wore me down as Swithin once did those in authority, and I suppose he's right. He has got what he desired, the girl he used to watch, only I'm a girl no more. I'm over fifty. I am an entirely different animal. I am no virgin quaking. I am no maiden weeping. I am no longer soil for planting. I no longer bleed. I haven't bled in years. My flesh is softer. It bruises easily, but my mind is harder. Perhaps once I could have been bent into a creature that resembled a wifely wife. Now, I am my own creation, and it's far too late to change me.

Around me, the crowd gasps in delight. Theophile has escaped the fires. The mummers have altered the script. I watch the Devil weeping. I cannot stop laughing. The applause is riotous. The play is at an end, but there will be another soon. Like the entire city, the mummers are trapped here until the Scots leave Ireland on their boats or breach Kilkenny's gates. We all wait for news, and in the meantime, I cannot go to the meadow. My sanctuary is the garden, and daily, when it rains, I sit beneath my mother's tree.

✿

At sext, I walk home to the inn. The meal is laid out in the dining hall. Large bowls of steaming bread rolls and thin cabbage soup. Guests mill about, some standing while scolding their children to sit. My new husband's two grown children swill about the room. The eldest son drowned more than thirty years ago—one less to deal with—and now there's only a married daughter, almost meaningless to a man like le Poer, and a son, attempting to reach forty in the next few years. The siblings drink and whisper and point about as if they're choosing which of my tapestries they'll take once their father and I are dead. I smile at them. Soon I'll convince le Poer to sign over his wealth to myself and Will, and then my smile will be so wide it will break my jaw. I haven't asked him. I never will. He must come to the idea on his own, assisted by my hints and Will's attention to him. I am close. I must be.

Now my husband sits on a grand chair which each of my spouses have perched on, but for him it looks the most fitting. He fills it with such ease. Always on first seeing him, I am intrigued by the chiselled jut of his chin and the lips which are slightly too large. His feet, bare inside his shoes, are propped on the table, ready to be whipped out and tucked beneath him while he sits. He is a man with bones loose-jointed, always wearing sumptuous furs and finely woven linens, none of which suit the brutish handsomeness of his face. He has the look of a labourer who ought to have died from tooth decay at age sixteen, and yet he ploughs on through the years, now reaching for sixty.

He crosses his hands behind his head. I cannot hear him, but I'm sure he gives a satisfied sigh. Will is stationed beside him, putting on a show of laughing and talking with emphatic hand gestures to mimic his new father, who nods, eagerly leaning in to hear my son's every word. Slowly, I approach, stopping to spare a few words for my neighbours William Payn de Boly and Alice Faber, who I usually avoid as they're simple people without much coin to their names and I trust neither of them; they are gossips and jealous of me. But my husband has thrown the doors open to them and anyone else local. I often find a clerk or the wife of a nobody sat at my table. Le Poer likes to have the place full and noisy, even if the company is dull. I laugh for William Payn de Boly, even though I was only half listening to his complaint about the butcher. I touch Alice Faber's arm, smile, and she beams back at me as if I gave her a bag of coins. Swiftly, I slip away, before either of them can grasp me and try to convince me I ought to invest in some foolish business venture one or other of them has begun of late. My seat is also carved, but by a more skilled craftsman than my husband's, the details of each flower more intricate, each one identifiable from the meadow; whereas his are imported flowers, carved by a man who's only seen drawings. The design of my husband's was chosen, of course, by my father.

"You look well, as always, wife," he says, waving a hand around casually. His mouth is full of over-chewed bread. He has turned it back to dough.

"You look well yourself, husband."

He grins and with seeming self-consciousness rubs his cheek.

"I just saw the play—"

He leans over me, grasps my breast and squeezes.

"Still so firm for a woman your age."

I cannot bat his hand away. I cannot bring the eyes of my guests to watch, because I know this hand of his will slap me, here, now, in front of everyone. He wants me to react. I know him now. Although it causes me a deal of focus I remain still and unresponsive.

"A lifetime of good food has kept me firm." I stare at him, making my face blank, and, as I have learned, he grows bored almost immediately and lets go of me.

"I shall tell a story," he announces to the room.

"Please do," Will says, giving me a pointed stare of pity. I look away.

Le Poer wipes his lips and taps his teeth until his audience is silent. His son yawns with exaggeration, and le Poer glares at him. I have noticed that there is little closeness between him and his children. I don't blame them, but I am also pleased by their folly. He is already more loyal to Will, who treats him like the father he always wanted, despite telling me he thought le Poer too volatile for me to marry. Yet my son is cunning like me, if on some occasions a little tactless. He knows how to make the best of any situation.

The guests are a mixture of wine merchants, a poorer trading family called Galrussyn and a few straggling churchmen who all share one room and over the past few nights have been noisy in their pleasure of each other. I avoid the eyes of my neighbours. There is something uncanny about having them beneath my roof on an ordinary day. Nothing good can come from our mixing with ordinary people, and I feel sure they will suffer for it more than me.

"As I'm sure you all know," my husband says, "my family are notorious for violence and lawlessness." He smiles and nods and again waits for silence, tap-tap-tapping his teeth.

"You all know what happened with Reginald Russell's wife, don't you? But you haven't heard it from my lips."

Someone brave might debate this statement.

"It was about five years ago now," he says.

"Six," I say.

"Is that so? My wife loves this story. So anyway, my nephew Stephen took it into his head that he fancied the look of the wife of Russell—and she was a looker. Brown curling hair down to here—yes, I am persuasive, I convinced her to show me. Anyway, when Stephen and I arrived with our men at the home of Russell, the coward fled, leaving his wife behind, but her reaction to us was, how should I put it, like a cornered deer. Stephen had said she was obsessed with him, but she didn't seem even to recognise my randy nephew. The imp had lied to me, and so I had no choice but to take her away from my relative myself. She was running. Hah. Poor woman thought she'd be fast enough to escape us. I got to my horse first. Stephen's men always take too much drink. I lifted her onto my horse and rode her—hush, don't laugh so at the woman's expense—to Dungarvan Castle. Stephen and his gang pursued me, but I am a good horseman. They couldn't catch up to us. He raged around outside the castle for a day, perhaps two—I was distracted and didn't keep count—anyway, he became bored and left at some point. It was six full days before Russell came to collect her. He wouldn't take her back until I swore on God's book she had not been dishonoured. I was keen to be rid of her at that point. The woman hadn't stopped crying, and we all know how wearying that can be, and so I agreed she was in fact a woman of good character."

"They called you to the court, did they not?" Will says.

Le Poer grins at my son, revealing a solid row of wine-reddened teeth. "They did. I was to give witness. Russell didn't believe she was untouched, and in his place I would think the same, but he was a bold man to question me a second time."

"You told them she was innocent?" I say.

"Like I just said."

"Out of kindness to her."

"But, of course."

"So it wasn't anything to do with preserving your name?" I asked.

He flashes me a smile. He enjoys the threat in my words.

"Would you not do the same, pretty wife? A name is power in this world of ours."

"You are right," I say. "I would lie too."

He laughs and leans in to speak to Will, surely some lewd words about me. I push away my soup. It has gone cold.

Her name is Margaret. I will always remember her. She was dragged through the courts. Her word was not believed. They heard from every man involved in order to decide if she was undefiled. Based on men's witness, the verdict was innocence. She was untouched, but short of killing my husband, I don't see how she could have kept him off her, and if she had murdered him, a man so rich, and her just a farmer's wife, she would have hanged for it.

Six nights and days with him. She knows there is a rage in him which flickers always just beneath the surface. On our wedding night, he bared himself in every way. He told me his first wife made him limp. He told me he was glad when she died. Then he stripped off his clothes and stood, arms out, smiling, as if he were offering me a great prize. I couldn't help it. I laughed. It was an instant, a flicker in his eyes, and he changed. His fist landed hard against my cheek, and I landed hard on the floor. The rest was a blur. He took me where I lay as if I were a servant. After, he wept, begged my forgiveness, said he would be gentle in future. I know liars, and I lied right back. I told him he would do as I say from then on. His tongue darted about his teeth, excited. I told him I would be his mistress, and for the most part, he has enjoyed doing my bidding, by day in business and by night in the bedchamber. Mostly, I have him under control, but, like a trained feral guard dog, sometimes he bites.

When he is snoring, I take to using a clay instrument of pleasure. Sometimes I think he's sleeping, but he laughs, and I jolt upright, sweat on my hands, and ask him what he finds so funny, and he says, you, you are funny, and he throws my pipe to one side and takes me himself, but these instances are better. I am prepared.

While I use my instrument, I think of Adam and I think of Richard. Sometimes, I think of Roger, and even rarer, I think of her, Margaret, a woman I have never met, but who knows my husband perhaps as well as I.

🌿 A Recipe for Poison 🌿

❖ When the night is at its blackest, leave the inn without a lantern. Over your arm carry a basket containing a trowel, a knife and a pair of shears.

❖ The month must be August or September.

❖ Make haste for the graveyard and go to your father's grave.

❖ Find the nearest yew tree and harvest six handfuls of berries, three branches and one root.

❖ Quickly, return to your kitchen, stoke the embers into flames, fill a pot with water and place it on the fire.

❖ Strip the leaves from the branches and squeeze the berries in your fists. Add the lot to the pot. Toss in the root. Wait for it to boil.

❖ At dawn, swiftly, without burning yourself, strain the liquid into an earthen pot and store it in your workroom. Behind a wooden panel will do. Leave it there to ferment. A month at least, but you can wait longer if you're able to withstand it.

❖ Once you're at your edge and no other option seems possible, add the liquid to your mother's vial and store it in the chest at the end of your bed, knowing each night that any morning you could begin administering it.

❖ For best results, add to pottage or wine.

❧ November 1317 ❧

I fear the world has no more miracles left for me. I fear I have eaten them all up, yet here she is.

She stands in the middle of my workroom on the fresh green rushes. Her brown eyes are bold, but her mouth trembles. Her nose is too large, yet her forehead is wide and only a little creased. The underarms of her tunic are stained yellow, but she stands with feet planted apart, arms crossed as if she doesn't care she's filthy, and, looking at her, I know I must have her. She cannot yet be over sixteen.

"My name is Petronilla," she says. "Petronilla of Meath. My child calls me Pet."

"You are married then."

"No."

"A widow."

"No." Her lips have formed a hard line.

"Well, Petronilla," I say, "you have the job, just so long as you will change out of those clothes. I have a few tunics I no longer wear. You may have them."

"Very well," she says, and I am captivated. She reminds me of myself at sixteen, myself if I had been born poor.

"My daughter, Sarah," she says, "she is four. She can work also."

"I am not charitable. I'm sure you've heard that about me."

Boldly, she holds my gaze, and I am almost undone.

"You may keep her with you," I say, "but you must feed her from your own plate."

Those bold eyes finally stare at the ground, and I think I have won, but she looks up and smiles.

"Even in Dublin, there is talk of you," she says.

❧

It is afternoon, and I watch them, Petronilla and her child tapping the frosted red berries of my mother's rowan tree. Petronilla looks well in my blue tunic. It heightens the cream softness of her cheeks. She seems to dance as she moves about, laughing so brightly I expect the ice on the river to shatter. She speaks with a deliberate slowness which can only be to teach the child to talk. She bends, picks up the little creature and tosses her into the frigid air. Although the child, Sarah, is small, I doubt I could throw her. Petronilla's body must be hard with muscle. Every step she takes looks to me as though her feet are rooting. Her child is sexless like all children, enraptured by the world around them, barely aware of the effect of their bodies on their parents. Their arms always reaching, hands fluttering for attention, grabbing, always grabbing, for their mothers' flesh.

Now, Petronilla grasps a large and pointed stone and slams it into a bucket, smashing the ice. Her daughter grabs a shard and waves it triumphantly, a knight with a sword. She runs, brandishing it, but freezes, dropping it on the path where it shatters into uncountable pieces.

Petronilla is already snatching the girl up, placing Sarah on her hip and striding back towards the inn, towards me. The child waves her hand about, dripping blood all over her mother's new tunic.

"Had enough of watching us?" Petronilla says.

"Your daughter isn't four," I say. "She's above two."

She shrugs. "You wouldn't take us if you knew she was so little."

Before I can answer, Petronilla marches into the inn, the child clinging to her, still sobbing and staring at me over her mother's shoulder. Her eyes are big and sad. It's as if she knows already the harshness her life will inflict on her bones and flesh. It's as if she knows her life and her mother's, like those of most servants, will be short. They will never reach my age, but then again, they will never see as much death as I have seen.

*

It's evening, and Petronilla is undressing my hair. Le Poer watches from the bed, chewing slowly on a chicken leg. There is no privacy with him. No solitary moments. Twenty years with William and he never once saw my hair, but on my wedding night le Poer tore off my wimple, and come morning there were red and grey strands tangled in his bunched fists.

He hacks into one of those fists. Perhaps signalling irritation at how long Petronilla is taking or perhaps for lust at watching me or her. I don't know, and nor do I wish to. I don't wish to delve into his mind, just as there are parts of my own I leave unexplored.

"I am going to get some wine," he says.

"Bring me some," I say.

He rolls off the bed and leaves the room.

Her hands stop plaiting my hair, and we are still and quiet, noticing how much larger the bedchamber feels now he is gone.

"I had a daughter once," I say. "She was prettier than yours, but not strong. She died before her fourth year."

"My daughter won't die."

"They all do. Eventually."

She continues plaiting my hair, tugging it. I don't close my eyes against the pain. I gaze at the distorted reflection of her in my polished mirror.

"Your husband, he—"

"You will get used to him," I say. "I did."

She raises one bushy eyebrow.

Outside, I hear icicles snapping and wonder does the river move under the ice.

"This is an inn," I say. "Keep your daughter in your bed."

Her hands pause on my head, and I sense she is readying to tell me something, but the door opens, and my husband enters. Behind him is a servant boy balancing a decanter and two wine goblets on a tray. He swiftly puts it down on the side table and backs out of the room. Le Poer laughs and pulls off his outer tunic. He opens and shuts his fist, a hint that he just punched the servant, but I doubt it. The boy is too fast and young for him. Le Poer only wants me to think he is in a battering mood, but I find more often than not that it is only the nights when he throws back too many goblets of wine and he cannot remain stiff that send him violent. But now, spritely, soberly, he leaps onto the bed and pats the blanket, glancing hungrily between Petronilla and me. Her hands clutch my head. I stand, approach the bed, tap my foot against my mother's wooden chest. The poison lies dormant inside. I could use it any day, if I chose. The warmth of her hands still clings to my scalp.

"Goodnight, Petronilla," I say, and she slips into the hall without a light, leaving le Poer and me all too visible in the flickering of the many lamps.

✹ December 1317 ✹

"Mama! Hungry."

People nod from beneath their ice-laden door lintels, but no one comes too close to Petronilla, Sarah and me, preferring the danger of falling frost daggers to us. All through Kilkenny the people whisper about me. They have always kept their distance, or perhaps I kept myself too superior to them. I have made myself unreachable. I have lost one too many husbands, even though many women over fifty have been widowed at least twice. I sense there's a low hum of hatred for me in the town, but I don't care. I don't need them. I have my friends. I have my son. I have my wealth, and now I have Petronilla too.

She leads Sarah over to a baker's window. I watch her ordering, paying and taking a loaf which she hands to the child.

"That baker can't be trusted," I say. "I hear his bread sends people wild."

"Well, that sounds like fun."

"I will buy better bread on the way home."

"I will decide what myself and *my* daughter eat."

But as we walk towards the city gates, she stops by a begging, wounded soldier and gives him the loaf.

"He's probably already driven mad by strange thoughts," she says.

In the meadow, I release her arm and run towards the trees. I hear her cackle and sense she is running after me. When I reach the forest I throw myself on the ground. She hurls herself beside me. Leaning on one arm, I look down at her face. Her eyes are shut. She's gone inside where I can't follow. I am tempted to press my panting mouth to hers, but I know she would only squirm away from me. I tell her of the skies I sometimes dream of: golden and bending towards a sea; lips tasting of sun; nightscapes with new stars. I tell her of the convent I visited when Will was still small, and of the illumination of two women outdoors, hair undressed, totally free, naked yet somehow safe. She laughs, calls me a beautiful fantasist, and Sarah looks between us, her mouth opening in surprise. I reach for her cap, but she jolts away.

"When I was about your age," I say, "I met a wildcat here."

Her eyes fill up with possibility. With her finger pressed to her lips, she creeps towards the edge of the trees, searching, growling softly, as if calling for a sister cat.

Petronilla examines my wrist. It is ringed with a purple bruise. It's two nights old but still stings. She presses it, harder than she needs, and I yank it back. She sniffs.

Without looking at her, I say, "I don't like to focus on it."

"I see that."

Every morning, I wake knowing I could end him, and the thought gives me strength. I could. He is in my hand, and I could crush him. But he hasn't yet changed his testament, and anyway, I have her, my free woman. She sees all and understands me. She gives me hope for lighter days and nights. With her at my side, I can go on here.

"I will teach you to read." I look up at her, expecting a bright, thankful face, but fear looks out from under her eyelids.

"What good would that do me? I am safer without the knowledge of that devilry."

"There is much joy to be got from it."

"And what joy have you gained from words?"

"Coin," I say. "Escape into other worlds."

She snorts. "As if I would get money for knowing words and other worlds? Sure, what's wrong with ours?"

"There's beauty and peace in the illuminations and words."

"Beauty and peace I'll get enough when I die. Believe me, if I did learn reading, it would cause me a deal of pain. I don't have your coins. I have no place in learning what you bankers and nobles and churchmen keep secret between yous. You may trifle with teaching me, but what happens when I move on to another household? How would they feel about my knowing how to read their money-books and books of fornication? No, no, I will keep myself as I am and steer clear of any taint of that sort from you. I prefer to lie under an open sky and laugh with my child."

"If you became a nun, you could read."

"And work myself and my child to the bone taking care of the rich nuns who gave their dowries to the church. No. Serving one lady is enough."

I laugh. "Fair point. You win."

Too soon we must leave the meadow. The sun has fled, and the sky's red bruise is turning purple. Behind us are the shadows of the trees. I feel the eyes of the creatures there. The hunted and the hunters.

🌿 A Kilkenny Tavern 🌿

"Didn't you hear what she did to me?"

"Lord, we're not ones to gossip."

"Could've fooled me. Have you not been whispering all evening about how the Kyteler woman had the whole court on her side. Course she did. Half of them are indebted to her. The other half have been in her bed."

"Sure, none of us here are over-fond of the lady, but would you talk of your own father's wife like that?"

"He was her victim. She was in league with the Devil, turning his mind against his children. He was old and sickening. Easy prey. It was all for his money."

"If you'd excuse me, lord, but I was understanding that she merely took you to court to retrieve her widow's dower. By law that's any wife's, even if the stepchildren should take against her."

"You think that's all she took? Oh no, before he died she had him change his testament to favour her and that weasel son of hers. And

her husband, he was bellowing laughing throughout the entire pro-
ceeding, his cousin, that Arnold le Poer, sat beside him sniggering
too, and no doubt he weighed in against me, and he about ready to
be Seneschal of Kilkenny. Who'd go against him?"

"You were very hard done by, lord. Perhaps you should have
weighed all this up before you decided to withhold her widow's
dower."

❧ October 1318 ❧

It is All Saints' Eve, and the sun is dying.

I light my bedchamber with many lamps and stare into the still water of my blackstone dish. In the reflection, my eyes burn with green flames. For a moment, over my shoulder, I see death's flickering black wing. I smile at my image. My husband has gone. He's been away four days, and no word, other than the usual rumours of violence and debauchery. I told him to go off and enjoy himself with his friends, and he, delighted, whirled me around, told me it was a tremendous idea and left. He is still so strong and brimming with energy, which I find steals my own, but now, I have all this space to gather and recoup.

There is a gentle tapping at my door. I leap up, hoping it will be Petronilla returned. She has only just left me for her own bed. I open the door, but instead of the slight frame of a woman, it's the familiar solid shape of a man. I should have known. Petronilla never knocks.

"Roger," I say, "what're you doing out after curfew?"

"I'll have to stay the night."

"Come down to my workroom."

I retrieve a lamp and follow his stooped figure down the stairs where the air is frigid. Our breath plumes before us. I should wake a servant to light the braziers, but I want to keep his arrival hidden, keep him just for me. We hurry to the kitchen, where I light a brazier to carry back and he finds beer and bread and cheese.

Like me, he has softened out over the years, but these past few months have worn new lines beneath his eyes. His wife died three moons ago. They lived in Dublin, as he is now Prior of Templar's seat in Kilmainham, and so I could only send him word that I was sorry. I never received a reply, but this late arrival, I suppose, is it.

In the workroom, I sit on the settle, but instead of joining me so our bodies might share a little warmth, he takes a chair on the other side of the room. He is too far from the brazier to feel its heat.

"Alice." He sounds so very tired.

I picture them, him and his wife, as I saw them once wandering through my garden, heads bent close together, almost appearing to be one person. Now, he is singular again, and how fragile he suddenly seems.

"Careful," I say. "Wait some years before you marry again when your judgement is sound."

"I am not you," he says.

"I haven't the fight in me for your honesty today, and nor, I suspect, do you."

He presses back each of the fingers of his left hand until they crack. He only wears one simple silver ring. Even though he's wealthier than most men, he doesn't display it on his person.

"You make so much noise," he says. "Even in Dublin. Your stepchildren."

"I know, I know," I say. "They want me dead. Nothing new there. Le Poer's are the worst, even though he's still living. They tell anyone who'll listen that I'm an adulterer. That I lie with animals. Cats, I believe."

"I'm not worried about that."

"I must say I didn't think them so imaginative."

He shakes his head, ignoring my joke. "They're spreading word that you killed Richard, le Blund and even my brother."

I sup my beer. "I have friends like you and the Seneschal of Kilkenny."

"Arnold le Poer's influence, and even mine, will only go so far."

"You will be Lord Chancellor before long."

He sighs, runs his fingers through his grey hair. "Joan said I should be wary about helping you."

"That bitch."

"Alice!"

"I trusted her."

"She didn't trust you."

"Well, she was wise. We both know that."

He smiles. His eyes have a far-off look.

"What was her reasoning?" I say.

"She thought you couldn't see beyond your own interest. You couldn't see, or didn't care about, the harm you would cause others."

"Well, she was right. I wouldn't have survived this long without my instincts to protect myself. It's what my father taught us both, but I couldn't work for the council like you. I had to find my own way in."

"I'm sure I'd have done the same if I were you."

"Aren't you going to say it's repugnant to see one so fair as me so unscrupulous?"

He shakes his head. "Sure, I know it would only fall on deaf ears."

"Too true. I'm far too old to change."

"You never would have changed."

"I might have," I say, "had I married you."

He smiles again, but in this moment, although he looks sad, it is with a hint of pity.

We sit a long while in silence until I tell him he must go lay his head in the house he has kept here all these years, and he agrees. The nightwatchmen would never arrest him anyway. Unlike me, he is above the law.

I step out into the garden in my bare feet to feel the frost. I don't want to return alone to my bed. I am cold. Everything is cold. I take deep, steadying breaths. They are gone. So many vanished from sight and only I am left to carry them.

My mother's tree has shed all her leaves. In the dark, I can only make out the topmost boney branches against the moon-washed sky. I still feel light from my husband's absence. My bruises are turning yellow. My limbs are my own. My hands are my own. I crack each finger, and it sounds like icicles snapping.

I press my ear to the trunk of the rowan tree, longing to hear her voice, her guidance, but this is childish. I am a woman, still young in body, despite my years, because I have supped well on meat and wine all my life, but my heart is withered beyond most. The tree's life beats a water-sap rhythm, even though the bark is mantled in ice. I know I wasn't meant to be a brief guest on this earth. I was meant to outstay my welcome, feasting a hundred years or more.

On the air, I hear two voices. A cat yowling in pain, a tom growling with pleasure. The prey and the predator. I have been both in my life. Perhaps I am always both, but just now I long to be neither. I long to sleep on a bed of moss, gazing up at open branches and a sky of uncountable stars, but I am not an animal. I need my soft mattress, my cakes and beer. I need to have my hair brushed by someone else's hands. I need the tender touch of silk. I am nothing without my workroom, my clients, my coin.

Lord! I am not yet wearied by the rising and dying and living. The smell of ice stings my nose. I hear the river creak beneath the shards. I could shout, if I wanted to, and hear my voice shoot across the water, before it travelled back, shattering ice. If I wanted, I could let loose my voice. I can have almost anything I want, except Roger. He is not mine. I see now he never has been. It is his loss, but it is also mine. Joan was gentle and kind and thoughtful. I am none of her, and I never could have been, but if he had married me, I would never have howled with the pain of loss and been so blinded by rage. Surely, I would never have feared the night, never feared myself. With him as my husband I never would have known the Devil so well.

I step back indoors, my feet heavy and numb.

Candle in hand, I take the stairs up to the top of the inn. I push open the familiar little door. Petronilla is curled in a ball around Sarah, shielding her from the cold.

I shake her shoulder.

"Get up," I say.

The child groans, sits up and rubs her eyelids. Petronilla's eyes flash in the light.

"I am cold," I say.

"And what do you expect me to do, mistress?"

I resist the urge to slap her.

"Come down. To my bed. And sleep at my side. So I won't be cold."

Petronilla climbs off the pallet and reaches for her daughter.

"She can stay here," I say.

Petronilla lifts Sarah onto her hip and passes me in a bustle of warmth.

"Sarah is coming with me," she says over her shoulder. "You said it yourself. This is an inn."

I follow them down to my bedchamber where they lie, shivering, curled against each other in my enormous bed.

🌿 Cooking 🌿

"She's a new thorn in her side."

"The new bishop, is it?"

"Stop your showing off, Petronilla. We also hear word of our mistress. Sure, it's spread all over town."

"What?"

"Witchcraft in Kilkenny."

"He won't be like the others, spending his days eating peacock and paying women to keep him stiff."

"But what if he's right?"

"Please. She's not a witch. There's no money in it. He's after her because the Pope pisses himself at the thought of witches, and so he says she's one, but he wants her because she's a good-looking, rich, old woman. He wants to punish her because she makes him question his virginity. Simple."

"You sound like her."

"So what. Don't you think she's right?"

"Suppose we'll find out."

❧ November 1318 ❧

St. Canice's Cathedral casts an enormous ice shadow over the graves. I am past my fifty-fifth year now, but most of the buried died before they reached forty. I plan to become a centenarian. There's no reason I shouldn't reach one hundred. I have all my teeth but one. Still, the darker half is now upon me, and I see it all about me. The year is tamping down to rest, pulling over itself the dead leaves and quiet frost. The cold has sent the Scots running. They have eaten up all our winter reserves. Now, guests for the inn will become rare and thin, but my household will see out the winter fine. Our stores are full of cured meats, wine, barrels of apples, pickled everything, sacks of flour and jars of honey. Today I am out in the cold to size up the man I haven't yet met but who already is obsessed with me.

I am being watched—that familiar sensation of gentle horror tingling the back of my neck. I suck in a breath, for a moment fearing it is my husband, but it can't be him. There's no reason he would climb the hill to St. Canice's, and anyway he'd never think to find me here on any day other than a Sunday when I have no choice.

I sense the watcher stands in the portico, but I don't look towards him. I don't give him the attention he wants because I haven't yet assessed his weakness.

I look up at the cathedral roof. One lone swallow peels her

wings and leaps into the air. She has been abandoned by her family. Perhaps she was injured, considered too weak to travel. Perhaps she was headstrong, thought she was tougher than them, but she shan't make it through the winter if she stays. Already, I can picture her plummeting from the sky, wings iced over.

I wait, and, under the close chimes of brass bells, the watcher finally reveals himself. He stands boldly, gazing out, not at me—at least he pretends not to—but at the graveyard, all Kilkenny's money-eyed dead. He could be speculating about how many coins he can still leach from them, but I doubt it. He has a particular prey in mind, one he's trying to lull, at this moment, into a sense of ease. Yet I am relaxed, and I know every hair on his little body must be standing on end because my eyes are on him. From this distance I cannot tell his age, but he seems neither old nor young. His clothes are those of a lowly Franciscan monk, but there is an air about him, a superiority, in defiance of his small stature, and it suggests that, despite being a stranger, he feels he owns this place. He can only be the new bishop.

Just as I decide to approach him, he turns and goes back inside the cathedral, and I am left wrong-footed, wondering if I ought to follow or if I should wait for the bustle of the cathedral after Mass when he's surrounded and must pretend some level of courtesy. I will wait. He expects me to run now to him. He wants me to come begging, to offer up a new glass window for the transept as a barter for his silence about my supposed dance with the Devil—clearly he has heard talk of my husband—yet sadly I can tell just from the look of him that he isn't witty enough to understand any humour, especially not from me, a woman. What he wants is for me to weep, to beg him to call off his whispermongers, but I refuse to give him what he wants. I too stride away from the graveyard. I know we will meet soon.

❧ A Bishop's Sermon ❧

"There are on this day, beneath this roof, those amongst you who are a seed of evil in Kilkenny.

Look about you and see your neighbours. The young mother who has delivered us so many of God's children. You know her: she feeds her babes from her own body. She works hard like all of you. Come night, she is spent, but she rests easy under the eyes of the Lord.

Now look about you. Ask yourself, do you trust all your family's hearts are good and pure as this woman's? Do your friends worship our Lord as they ought? Or are they consorting with those forces who would turn them away from the church? You know they are in your midst: the debauchers and usurers, the old women, the poisoners.

Look! Pay attention. They're there. Sat beside you. Pretending their innocence. Don't be fooled by their beautiful faces. Or their honeyed words. The Devil was an angel; to look on him you think you are seeing Heaven, but to the untrained eye Hell and Heaven may at first appear alike. Guard yourselves.

And remember, I am an ear, always listening for you whenever you sense them leading you astray. I will save you, if only you will come to me swiftly, before you are turned."

⚛ November 1318 ⚛

All my life when I have seen a man performing in the guise of himself I have always seen absurdity or cruelty. This little Franciscan, this
new Bishop of Ossory, Richard Ledrede exhibits both, and I cannot
help but think the two combined can be nothing except dangerous,
yet I am struggling to find it possible to fear him. I have seen more
bishops buried than I can count. He will be as fleeting as the rest.
On this Sunday, he wears matted and oily black fur made from an
animal I can't identify. He drags the pelts behind him as he paces,
proclaiming his message of fear in a surprisingly loud and booming
voice. I look forward to telling neighbours he is in need of a flagon
of wine, a rich meal and a good fuck. They will agree but tell me
that unfortunately for him, and all of us, like most of his Franciscan
brothers, he will deny himself all life's sweetness in the hopes that
the Lord will gift it to him in the afterlife. Beside me, my husband's
yawn is loud, and it draws those piercing little eyes to us. Ledrede has
an expression of repugnance which I enjoy and loathe equally. I stare
back at him, and he looks away, his pasty skin bruising red. He wants
my attention, and yet fears it.

Le Poer gazes about the cathedral, searching for friends to distract him. He is liked by most, all those susceptible to his generosity
and infectious need for festivity. It is almost endearing, his need for

validation from his acquaintances. My inn is truly the best place for him, because nightly a different guest is there to listen to him talking about his exploits, his wealth, his contacts. A wine merchant's wife tells me it is heartening to see a couple who are so similar, but she blanches when she sees my face and says we're similar in only the best sense: our joviality and enthusiasm for life. I laugh her off, and she rushes away. She was wrong. He and I are different in almost every way. He is sweet where I am ruthless. He is violent where I am gentle. He is lusty where I am cold, and where I am passionate he is uninspired. Yet still I find I like him as often as I loathe him, and I know he feels the same for me. We are a well-matched pair after all. But there is one gap. He doesn't see the threat of the Franciscan. He sees the short man as a subject to laugh about over wine, as do I, but unlike le Poer, I always taste the danger. I must. The tiny bishop nurtures a passionate spite for me, and from his pulpit he could poison everyone with it.

Petronilla's hand darts into my lap. I take it and squeeze. Her shoulder shakes against mine. I shush her, holding in my laughter.

To my left, my husband leans in close to my ear. "The new bishop is hard for you, wife."

I touch the back of my neck before he can and find a strand of hair has escaped my cap.

Graveyard. Wind-whipped. Children running for home, and parents trudging after them.

I hang back inside the cathedral portico, waiting for Ledrede. I have sent Petronilla on with my husband. I thought she would be eager to return to the braziers, but also I wanted to approach the bishop alone, without a young woman distracting his attention. It has been long enough that we have skipped around each other. Now is the day to meet, especially as I sense he doesn't wish to confront me while his plan of destruction is still vague.

I watch Petronilla and Sarah rushing to keep up with my husband's swift pace. At the edge of the graveyard, both Petronilla and the child turn, gazing back at me with forlorn expressions. I look away and enter the cathedral again.

*

"Bishop."

Ledrede jumps at the sound of my voice, and I regret my loudness. My bold approach is not correct for him. To have made him comfortable, I ought to have knelt, pretended to be caught in prayer, so he might have approached me from a height, a stance of importance, and felt domineering. Instead, he now darts a look up at me, his arms loose and skittish, and newly I feel judged and feared by this little man, but I don't want to put him at his ease. Ossory comes with vast wealth and influence, yet I am almost as rich and still better connected in our city than this stranger. He can feel my power just now, sense his mistake in tampering with my reputation.

"What is it you require?" he says. "I cannot tarry long."

"Those Latin hymns we sang," I say, "you composed them, didn't you? I am an admirer of art in all its forms."

"They were my composition. Yes. The words and the melody."

"You made Kilkenny's nobility sound like songbirds, rather than the coop of chickens I fear we truly are."

His stiff stance shows me why the Pope chose him. Unlike his meaty predecessors, all too susceptible to calls of the flesh, this bishop is stone. I have done business with all his lecherous predecessors. Each one handed over a small fortune of the Lord's coin in loan repayments just so they could luxuriate at vast expense before their deaths, but I can tell he won't pilfer away the holy coin, at least not to me.

"I hope," I say, "that your compositions will dissuade our clergy from singing secular songs."

"These local songs are full of devilish persuasions."

"You are so talented, I would love to see your visions performed outside the cathedral walls. Would you never put your hand to a play?"

"To make a joke about such a matter for a man in my position is debasement."

"Forgive my uncouthness," I say. "I am not used to a man in your position with, let's say, your unsullied character. But do tell me, did our dear Pope enjoy your writings. I feel sure myself he often requested your hymns—"

"Well, yes, but—"

"And read a poem or two of yours before bed."

"Mistress le Poer—"

"Excuse me, bishop, but I am in fact, and I hate to bring it up, a dame."

"I am aware of all your marriages."

"Excellent. My reputation has spread as far as France."

"You are proud of your notoriety."

"Notoriety, my pious bishop, is good for business."

He stares up at me, a feral expression in his eyes, but in all other regards his face remains neatly pious. I finally break his gaze, and he says, "I know all about you—"

"You cannot trust my stepchildren."

"*They* don't soil their hands with usury."

"No, they only wish to profit from it. As this very cathedral has done since my father's day. Do you think the Marshalls could have paid for all these stones, if they hadn't borrowed from people like me?"

A wash of sunlight pierces the window above, casting coloured light all around us. Yellow and orange. A bath of light or flame. I smile at him, and the stiffness of his jaw tells me he knows I paid for this vision. He swallows his spite, nods and strides away from me.

I have made a little enemy today, but I cannot find it in myself to care much. I will crush him as I have countless other men.

❧ The Inn's Kitchen ❧

"Did you?"

"Did you?"

"He's the worst of them."

"I liked the last."

"You mean you lay with him?"

"Oh no. He'd have never betrayed the mistress. That's why I liked him."

"With this one, she doesn't care, even if he kills us."

"To them, we're no better than animals."

❧ October 1320 ❧

A beautiful stranger is carrying a flute. In the light of the lamps hanging from the beams, his dark skin has a blue sheen like the River Nore in winter. He is a water I could set sail on.

A Marshall cousin whispers to me that the musician looks like a demon. I tell the man that being born under a warmer sun than ours does not make a man a demon, and anyway I have seen a demon, and he was not so beautiful. The Marshall baulks and sidles away, and I am left laughing alone. It is so easy to frighten a man away when you are an old woman, but heads still turn to look at me laughing, their eyes, admiring, yellowish in the lamplight.

Lately, I have felt I am walking down a path I can't see, a bell in my hand, proclaiming my location, and all the while I sense a flame at my side, hot, tantalising and a little dangerous. The musician senses it too. With his flute pressed to his lips, a quick light tune issuing from the reed, he approaches me and, removing the instrument from his mouth mid-tune, asks, "Lady, what is your favourite food?"

"Lovemaking."

His dark eyes widen. Later I could meet him in my workroom. Oh, life without tomorrow's day, that is how I wish to live this night, even as I feel le Poer's hand land on the back of my neck and draw me across the room so I can barely hear the music any more.

In my workroom later, the flautist will whisper so many meaty words. I could kiss his bare, moist shoulders and between kisses tell him of my great wealth, but for now my husband has a hot grip on me, and I must talk to all his vile, drunken friends. Worst of all, I have lost one shoe. I slap le Poer's hand from my neck and tell Petronilla that when the party's over she must take the hand of the flautist and lead him to my workroom. Her eyes widen in shock, but she laughs and nods. She can yet live.

I drink more wine and have a bitter thought that my red shoe will be tried on by everyone at the party, making it misshapen and unwearable by me in future.

❧ Paradise ❧

It is no garden. No, it is not cut into geometric forms. Nor do cages entrapping songbirds hang from tapered trees. Truly, despite what the churchmen say, flowers do not grow in neat rows.

No, no, it is a forest and a meadow. It is the place where the hawk hangs waiting for a sight of the mouse. It is the long grass where poppies bloom and wave like red flags. Here, the dog rose leaps skywards, the wind shaking out its gentle scent and the thorns catching the fur of a wolf. Here, moth larvae nick away at bark until trees crash to the ground, and snow falls, suns set and rivers change course. It is the place of great sky-shattering storms. A place where two women could stand naked, hair undressed for the wind to dance.

❧ April 1321 ❧

Petronilla and I walk in the dark, rubbing the sleep grit from our eyes, carrying lanterns to guide our way along the riverbank. On her back, tied up in a blanket, she carries our bread, kneaded and baked in our own oven. These days, all I seem to hear beyond the rumblings of the little Franciscan about my love of demons are reports that people are raving, strange and dark fantasies pouring from them when they eat the bad bread sold in half Kilkenny's bakeries. I cannot have my guests falling ill or, worse, dying, their purses dying with them. I cannot have my servants made wild and irrational. And, most frightening of all, I cannot have Petronilla, the stable thing that keeps me rooted and surviving, losing her nerve.

Petronilla leads. I follow with only my flame and my thoughts. When we reach the pebbled beach, the morning is a cool blue. We are surrounded by the tall rushes and the damp stones. The trees grow close to the water, hiding us from anyone passing on the road. Facing the river, Petronilla pulls off her cyclas and under-tunic. Her body is a flash of white against the grey stone. Her belly is too round and too beautiful. Soon the babe will be born, and her stomach will sag and flatten. Today, she looks as though she's swallowed the brightness of the world, but her smile is like a knife. It's not for me. She gives it boldly to the sky, the river, the day ahead. I hate her for it and yet I love her. I long, heartily, to be this girl, this mere servant, swimming in rivers, lying with whoever she pleases and, at night, nestled in a child's embrace.

Whooping, she walks into the river and briefly disappears, before her small head reappears on the black surface.

"Come in," she calls, but I cannot. I am stuck in my mud-encrusted shoes on the hard ground. I cannot float, and I cannot admit it to her. Instead, I rest against an oak and watch her swing back her arms, cascading water. I long for her to return to shore. I long to pass plums between our hands and brush flies from each other's cheeks. I even long for her to vanish beneath the surface; I would rush down from the bank, run into the water, find that I swim like a fish and pull her out to safety. I watch her and watch her, floating, arms whipping out now and then to right herself, to push herself back up against the current. She cares nothing for the thought of being seen by me or anyone. She basks in the grip of the cold water. She whoops and turns onto her back, quenching all sounds, even me. I see the white globes of her already milk-hardened breasts. She is strong and still so very young. She will make it through the birth. She will.

I call her name over and over until finally her head glides upright. She waves, and I beckon. Slowly, as if her body is suddenly heavier, she pulls her glistening self out of the water, and quickly I throw my cloak around her.

"We're going back," I say.

"What about the bread?" But her voice is weak and unconvincing.

"You've tired yourself. We'll eat on the road back."

Her face is drawn and pale. She nods and leans heavily on the arm I offer her.

All the way back to Kilkenny I feel as if we are being dogged by some malevolent follower, but when I turn to look, there's only the brown road.

"Promise me," I say, "if you are ever hit by lightning and catch fire, you'll run into the river and swim."

She shakes her head. "And what if I can't reach the river?"

"I'll carry you to it."

◢

We get bold looks all the way down St. Kieran's Street. Petronilla clings to me. All her strength has been stolen by the river.

"Almost there," I say over and over, but the words have become a chant, rhythmic yet meaningless. She must think we will never return to the inn and she will die in this shit-trodden Kilkenny street, but then we do make it to the side entrance, hobble across the plank bridge and through the garden door, leaving it wide open. I bring her into the kitchen, instruct my strongman to carry her up to her room and tell the cook to prepare her a warm drink, some broth and more bread.

I watch my strongman carrying her along the hall, her white face appearing tiny over his broad shoulder. She looks so small. I have never, until today, seen her look afraid. I turn away, rush down the hall towards the garden.

◢

The smell of rosemary and lavender fail to mask the scent of some dead thing rotting in the heat. Cats of every hue sunbathe and roll about in the herbs.

I walk down to my mother's tree. I stand on the river's edge, watching pink petals glide by. I don't have to wait long for him. I don't turn, but allow him to come up beside me, let him think he has the upper hand. His shadow falls on the water, making him appear taller than he is.

"Good day, bishop," I say without looking at him. "To what do I owe this visit?"

"This town is a hotbed," he says.

I suspect he doesn't know why he is here and is still composing a reason to give me.

"The weather," I say, "should be cool for you in autumn, but I am surprised—was Avignon not hotter?"

"The weather is not what I was referring to."

Panting slightly, he shakes his head. I offer him a drink from my waterskin, but he refuses it. A cat rubs against his leg. He bends and pets it. The cat purrs, rubbing harder against him.

"I often wonder," I say, "if our life's experiences had been different, would we act differently?"

The bishop straightens, his expression strained as if he were squatting over the shit pot but can't get his longed-for release. The cat continues to circle his feet. "All God's children," he says, "are on their path. There are no ifs."

"And, in your view, can they all be saved?"

"Of course."

"Even the usurers and the witches?"

His head snaps towards me. "Only if they are repentant. Are you repentant?"

"Did you ever dream of having a wife, bishop?"

Ledrede blanches. "Never."

"You surprise me."

There is a pleasant wildness in the snarling shape of his mouth.

"Today, along with me, you watched my servant bathing in the river," I say.

He gives a sharp inhale. I turn so I am directly facing him.

"I have often thought," I say, "I would have done better if I had been born a boy, and you yourself have many qualities admired in women, don't you think? Your stature for one, but more than that. Your person. When you speak on the subject of witches, women, old women specifically, you speak with such unmasked passion— the kind of fire any husband would wish his wife possessed—and yet your voice has such a delicacy. You would pass by day as sweet and gentle. You are the perfect woman, Ledrede; if only you had been born unarmed like me, you might have made many men's lives blissful."

A rash of red spreads across Ledrede's cheeks.

I touch his arm. He stares at my bare hand on his sleeve and shudders. I cannot help myself. I laugh.

He shakes off my hand, opens his mouth and clamps it shut again.

He bustles down the garden, and I laugh again and again and again.

❧ May 1321 ❧

Petronilla moos. Her legs buckle, but Sarah and a red-cheeked servant girl catch her arms. I smell the tang of the liquid as it bursts from between her legs. I rush forward, drenching my feet, and catch the baby as it falls out. Its hair is dark with blood. The eyes are large and black and shining. I look between the plump legs. A girl. All of her is pudgy, even though she is so new. Unlike her daughter, Petronilla's arms are floppy, her eyes glazed. She is gone from her body, at least for now. I instruct Sarah to lie beside her and tell the servant to press Petronilla's breasts until yellow beads drip. I take them on my finger, popping them in the baby's mouth. Petronilla falls asleep, Sarah curled against her, and the servant rushes off—no doubt heading for her own pallet—and so I wrap the baby girl in a green silk scarf and take her with me.

I carry her about the garden, show her the lilac and the rosemary, the thyme and, lastly, the rowan tree, weighed down with white blossoms, but this sweet babe, still so light, she cannot yet see; even when I bend and kiss that little forehead, she doesn't yet know I'm not her mother.

She bellows for her mother's breast, and I wish on my dead mother's tree that I was not so old and could feed this child myself.

Still, as she screams I stay beneath the rowan, watching the blossom sway against a bluer sky than yesterday's. I know soon I will return her to the mother who made her, but for now we stay here, her screaming and me smiling down. Her shrieks fill the air with sparks. Her voice warms my skin, singes it. I cannot stop my smiling. I cannot help but feel summer's warmth on my skin.

🌿 A Lullaby 🌿

Look up now and see
The stars, they are dying
That light, see, it's fading
A night thick with moths
Wing against white wing
Alive but just for the night
O do sing them your song
Of a life lived with feet
Buried in the damp soil
And bent towards the sky
A life rooted and uprooted
A time silent and screaming
Inside and inside out.

❧ August 1322 ❧

I tear apart last year's bread and scatter it in the garden for the birds. Perhaps they will all be maddened by the mould in it and, turned against each other, rip out their neighbour's feathers, leaving all of them flightless, stuck for ever in my garden. The servants have already thrown their bread about, so the ground is pulsing with starlings, sparrows and fat pigeons, pecking about for the dry scraps, all goodness and life gone from the old crumbs. It is Lammas, first fruits, when we throw out the old bread to make way for the new. The little Franciscan has banned any celebration of the first harvest inside the churches because it's too joyful, but there's no holding people back. I can hear laughing in the street beyond. There's no need for a priest. Every house can thank the earth themselves.

Petronilla is on the riverbank, tossing the bread to the ducks paddling against the pull. The babe, Basilia, is balanced on her hip. She is a flower of a child, words already blooming from her lips, even though she's only just over a year. Her dark eyes drink in all she sees with an air of superiority that rivals even my own. She is brown-skinned like her flautist father but a shade lighter, her cheeks pink with the summer and hair pale like her mother's. I am decided Basilia will not labour a short, painful life. I will save her from that. I have written them both into my testament, small favours compared to what is destined for Will, but more than any servant or servant's child has ever known.

Will is at their side. He's here to tell me what new whispers pour from the cathedral doors across the city. This is the cycle now between us. He comes to deliver rotten news, and I wait to receive it. A secret rage at me is boiling in him. I see it in the twist of his lips when he tells me the bizarre tales the little Franciscan shares with his priests about me, and the priests, as all churchmen do, spread cruel words faster than any baker. It is all fanciful. It is all meaningless, except people have taken up the whispers and seem now to believe them. They say I am a witch, and this would never have mattered before the little Franciscan came, except now he tells them and his slimy priests that witches are in league with the Devil. Still, all the talk is mostly hushed. It may yet blow out like a candle if there is nothing to grasp in the stories, and I have made sure that many other names are also circled by the whispermongers. Neighbours and acquaintances I chose almost at random. Those who irritated me. Those who didn't repay a loan. Those who happened to have crossed my path on the day. I told a servant or my strongman a tendril of gossip I wanted spread.

I watch as Will picks up Basilia and the child bashes his face. Petronilla leans in to stop her daughter beating the mistress's son. All three heads are close together, almost touching. For a moment, they appear like a family, and I want to scream. I wave to them, but none of them look up. They are laughing together. The sound frights the ducks into the air. Will hands Basilia back to her mother and strides up the path towards me, and I am hit, as I so often am, with the shock of his great height, his beard, the crinkles around his eyes as he smiles. He bends and kisses me, and I must reach up and touch his head to prove to myself that he is real, that this man is my baby.

"Careful, Mother," he says. "Behave."

"And what is it you suspect me of?"

He winks and presses his cheek to mine and says, "Now, I have the pleasure of paying my respects to my false father so he might pay me for my loyalty."

He pulls away and, whistling, enters the inn.

I walk down towards Petronilla and Basilia. They appear so small against the surging river. Petronilla is staring downstream, attention caught on a leaf that's floating away, but Basilia waves one fat fist in my direction. She opens her fingers to reveal a coin. I snatch it. She could swallow it and choke. Will must have given it to her. He ought to have his own children so he would know. Basilia roars with rage as I bend to pick her a golden water lily.

"This is better," I say as I hand it to her, but she tosses it back at me and, after a brief, furious pause, laughs.

Petronilla is still gazing out at the water. Her profile, one eye wide and bright, cheek red but fading and her wimple slightly skewed, is, all at once, simple and wild. Just now, she is untranslatable into any language, and I know I will never really understand her, yet she, I fear, may see me better than I see myself.

"I want you to marry Felix," I say.

She shakes her head as if she's trying to wake up. "You would sell me to a man you employ to draw blood for you?"

"Being unwed, it's dangerous."

"And the marriage bed is safe?" she says, finally turning to face me. Her face is too calm, unending in its judgement.

Basilia tugs at her wimple. I lift her from her mother's arms, feel the solid wriggle of her as she adjusts. She is a strong child. She must make it to adulthood. I squeeze her, and she squeals. I apologise in a whisper, and we both look out at the water that her mother's eyes are fastened to. I wish we were all at the bend in the river, her damp from swimming and us lying back in the sun. If we were there, I might tell her anything. I might tell her it's not so simple, it was never planned. If we were on the riverbank, I might forget my standing and kiss her, but we are here, where cats are yowling in the street beyond and in one of the sleeping chambers a child is weeping; and here we stand on the stone path that I own and she does not.

The sun is setting. The river is broken shards of red light. I nuzzle my face into Basilia's neck. She squeals, and I pass her back to her mother. Petronilla's eyes are too lucid, lit with a terrible spark. Her gaze is steady, curious, without fear.

She takes my free hand, and for a while it's just the three of us, watching the river race away from us to the sea.

*

Men's voices in my workroom. The door swings wide. Will is standing just inside, looking back into the room, laughing, but he turns towards the door, to me who he doesn't yet know is in the corridor. The laugh falls from his mouth. His eyes are cold and furious, and, on seeing me, his lips firm into a hard line. He nods, steps into the hall, places a firm hand on my shoulder and strides towards the street door. I know le Poer was speaking of me, and his words will have been vulgar. In order to reconcile my superiority in business, he must rate me for my woman's body, for the tricks I perform on him to keep him tied to my house.

He is sat now on my chair, his feet propped on my table. My ledger lies open. He is, in this moment and every moment, reviled and acclaimed by everyone who knows his name, but, by me, he is neither, except when in his presence I debase myself in my own heart by telling exaggerated stories about his valiant deeds to clients I wish to impress. He runs his fingers through his thick pelt, all shades of black and grey. Strangely, I want to rub my own hand over his head, whisper cooing noises into his ears and have him place his head on my lap, licking goose fat from my fingertips. I approach him, leaving the door wide. He doesn't flinch when I push first one foot and then the other off my table, and they land with thwacks on the floor. He grabs my wrists and yanks me towards him. He wants me to sit on his lap, and so I do. It is poignant, sweet even, how he dances between wanting to be wanted and wanting to assert his authority over me.

"I could end you," he says with the smile of a child.

"You don't have it in you," I say, "but I do."

He laughs as if I'm joking, as if it's impossible for a wife to be a threat. I laugh too. I laugh because he is adoring and vicious all at once. I could bite him, but instead I shut my eyes and await his kiss. With him, inhabiting moments like these, I do feel like a girl again.

❧ Whispers and Shouts ❧

"Fat on our coin."

"Bitch."

"Cat, more like."

"Bitch's taken all my father's coin from me."

"We'll get it back and more."

"She fought me for the widow's dower."

"I'm not saying it will be easy."

"But she's a murderer. Surely—"

"No, you've not been listening. She's a witch."

"But—"

"The bitch is a witch."

"So what?"

"Think, man. The bishop."

"So we're saying she's a witch then?"

"Yes!"

❧ December 1323 ❧

Christmas Eve

Kilkenny is frozen in a crystal night. The moon's sickle is paler than bone. I am pacing the streets, caring not for the dangers of men armed with drink and greed and gossip; such creatures will ignore me, a woman past twenty. From beyond the river I sense a snowstorm coming. Behind the shutters and animal skins, the faint glow of other people's lights. Kilkenny rings with bells, proclaiming the news of the Child born unto a virgin. I spit on the ice. Virgin, indeed.

I enter the inn and find it's silent, except for the hushing noise silence holds to your ear. Tonight, there are no guests, and the servants are all in bed. I climb the stairs with heavy feet. Opening my bedchamber door, I expect dark, but it is brightly lit with many lamps. I am meant to see him—I am sure he planned it—his broad, white, meaty back and, peeking from beneath his shoulder, Petronilla's face.

I am pulled to leave, but I stay in the open doorway, looking at Petronilla crushed beneath my husband.

He groans, climbs off her and slaps his naked belly.

"I'm getting a drink," he says, pulling on his many tunics.

"Bring me a cup," I say, stepping into the room so that he may step out.

He grunts and slopes through the doorway.

Petronilla has crawled out of the bed. She is still fully dressed. She hasn't noticed her wimple has crept too far back, revealing her light hair. I step towards her, to straighten it for her.

"Don't touch me." She's looking through me.

"Pet, I—"

"I know what I am doing." Her face, so still and set, is spectacular. She speaks through gritted teeth. "This is an inn."

These words are a fire in my mind. Of course, I had smelled it about him, but I pushed it away. I kept Basilia with me all day, knowing Petronilla had her safe at night, and Sarah, who worked now in the kitchen, slept still with her mother. They were safe. I had known the girls were safe, but I hadn't thought of Petronilla. She was old enough to protect herself, but I forgot she isn't me. All she has is her own body.

She's already leaving me, going to her children. I know she must. She is their protector. There is a vastness between us, and he has made it so. Her face tells me she will never speak about this night or any like it. Her hard, straight lips are a knife, meant for me, and I am terror. I am rage.

*

Christmas Day

I mix the yew extract into my husband's bowl of pottage. He sees my hand stirring but doesn't even blink before lifting his spoon to his smiling mouth. He trusts me, even with all he knows of me. With each mouthful he confirms his own vanity, and I realise I planned his death the moment I unmasked the goat, the day I heard what was done to Margaret, the evening I met his first wife. This is the meaning I give to my hand that stirs.

After eating his pottage, he kisses me, and I have to pull away to stop his poisoned tongue entering my mouth.

"Not here," I tell him.

"Just one nibble," he says.

I offer up my neck, and he bites. I make no sound even as his teeth drag.

"Later," I say.

"You're killing me," he says, but I can't laugh.

$\mathscr{q}$

Wren's Day

All night, amidst the sounds of violent expulsion, he groans behind the screen. I should have thought to light incense to flavour the air.

Early, I am woken by strawboys knocking on the inn's door in search of a coin for the wren. They are so flammable, stuffed as they are with dry grass. Likely they'll set all Kilkenny alight in their search for one tiny bird. I leave my husband and descend to my workroom. Basilia is tucked close to the brazier, blowing on her small fingers. Petronilla must have left her here for me, but she, the mother, is nowhere to be seen. I cannot help but draw the child onto my lap.

"The boys hunt the wren because they say she betrayed the son of God. He'd run through a field, and as he ran drops of his blood fell on newly sown wheat, and miraculously, to cover his tracks, the grain all shot up to full height. The wren flew up from the wheat singing, showing the soldiers where he had gone. The wren must die for the year to end, and those boys are the ones who will kill her."

Basilia takes this in, wide-eyed. Sometimes I think she is a little afraid of me.

❧

Holy Innocents' Day

"Do you think people like me?" he asks me.

"People?"

"I am unwell, but no one comes. Not even my children."

"But my Will visits."

"You did write to them?"

"Your children? Yes. Several letters."

"I have been thinking."

"Don't strain yourself."

"I'm changing my testament."

"How sweet you are. I'll get a clerk."

❧

The bells of St. Canice's are muffled, weighing the day with sadness. I walk through town towards the cathedral. In every house, people pray and weep supposedly for the babes Herod murdered, but it is their own they mourn, the lost children and the children yet to be lost. We are all here on this soil to protect our children in whatever way we can.

❧

In the cathedral I blow a kiss to the stained-glass face of St. Margaret. She is my warning. She was the daughter of a pagan priest, but after her mother's death she was nursed by a Christian. She reached girlhood, and a Roman governor demanded she marry him, but she refused. She wouldn't give up her faith, not even for a rich man. She never learned the art of persuading men to believe they are in charge, and this was her unravelling. If she had wanted to escape, she should have lied and told him she would marry him, then in the darkness of night fled before he could get his hands on her. In the end, because she was stubborn, the Roman beheaded her.

I know the Franciscan is standing behind me. I turn, and immediately we stare at one another, assessing, sizing. His tongue flicks in and out, worrying at the left corner of his mouth where there is a flaking patch.

What I see: terrified bully hungry for sainthood.

What he sees: insatiable, man-eating witch.

Both of us are accurate in our assessments. Both of us see danger.

It is mere moments of looking, but each moment pulls like a tooth extraction. I pass him slowly, smiling with teeth, and with teeth he answers my smile.

"Sarah sleeps with a red shoe."

Petronilla is barefoot. I wish I had more rugs on my workroom floor. The blue veins on her neck and hands stand out.

"It's been years," I say. "I threw out the other."

Petronilla nods.

"I caught him," Petronilla says. "He was looking in your storage chest."

She bends and scoops up Basilia from the floor. She is turning away from me, facing the door. She has stolen herself from me, yet loathsomely appears often, eyes looking always down, never up at me. Yet I can't hate her. She seems still so young. She can't know what she would've done if she was me. No one could.

"Are you all right?" I say.

"He sent me out of the bedchamber," she says. "I waited, watching, and two priests arrived and left. They had bags."

"To be carried to the little Franciscan."

"Yes."

"Come here," I say.

She shakes her head and readjusts Basilia on her hip, who is straining now to climb down, too full of life to remain captive, even in her mother's arms, for long.

"Please," I say.

Petronilla turns now, face bold with a look of hate, yet open and helpless too. No gratitude for my saving her and her daughters.

"Now you see me," I say.

I wish she would speak so I can refute each word of judgement, but there it is. She is silent, Basilia's arms around her neck. She leaves me. If she stays, it will only be because no one in Kilkenny will hire her and the roads are impassable with snow.

Already rage drags its fiery tail over my limbs. I long to run.

⌀

So tall, I stand above my husband. He is shrunken, near swallowed by our marriage bed. His hair has all gone, save for one small clump above his right ear. He is become an infant again, bald and mewling. His scrawny hand reaches from beneath the blanket. Half the nails have fallen out. I stare at them, disgusted and entranced.

"Get me the priest," he says.

I wait, examining my own fingernails.

"Please," he says.

"Do you have another confession?"

For some reason, I can't stop smiling.

"I told him," he says.

"Told who what?"

The candle sputters in my hand.

"The priest," he says. "Poisoning me. You."

"Ah."

"Ledrede has plans . . . nice man . . . after all."

"The Franciscan was here?"

"So many plans."

⌀

It's night, and I go one last time to see my husband.

Cold, he is turned away from me.

ALICE

❧ Accusations ❧

"She denied the faith."

"Not just her. A bunch of women. Some men too."

"For a year and a day."

"Dismembered animals."

"Scattered the parts at a crossroad."

"For their demon."

"Robert, son of Art."

"I heard he was Robin."

"A bird."

"No, the demon."

"Broke into St. Mary's."

"Whispered curses against their own poor husbands."

"Extinguished candles."

"Shouted: *Fi! Fi! Fi! Amen.*"

"Used powders and ointments to entrap us."

"Entrails of cocks."

"Dead men's fingernails."

"The brains of unbaptised boys."

"Over a fire of oak logs."

"All cooked inside the skull of a thief."

"The dame Alice mated with the demon."

"It was a black man."

"No, a dog."

"They had an iron rod."

"She rides it every night."

"And here was I thinking she just killed her husbands."

❧ January 1324 ❧

No one comes to meet me with a lantern. I have to find my way home by a yellow-tinged moonlight. Now he is dead, I cannot sleep in my bed. Beds are where you die, not live. The plank bridge over the shitbrook creaks at my tread. Usually the door is locked from the inside, but it opens. Any thief could break in and steal whatever they wanted. Now he is dead, I possess so much worth stealing. I have all I need, and this makes me empty. I think of trees and two women naked. I listen for the calls of evil birds. The Franciscan has turned the city of my birth against me. He wants to feast on my shame, but I won't let him. He will merely hear me thunder and remember me with rage. In the weeks to come, he will look up, and the rim of the sky will be crimson, and he will wish I hadn't lit him on fire.

The garden is silent. All life is gone. Petronilla stands beneath the rowan in the shade of its loving branches. Pressed against her side is Sarah. I long to go to her, to wrap my arms around her, but I stand back and watch, half expecting her to leap into the river, bringing Sarah with her. But she doesn't. She has no need to. She's not on fire.

Roger,

Throw this letter on the flames once you've read it.

The accusations against me are all just proof the little monk hasn't got it off in years. Just my luck, to be cursed with a poet for an enemy.

I know you think he writ the charges before he chose me as his victim, and you are right: they bear a resemblance to the case brought against the Templars in France but allow me my vanity. It's me he so passionately despises.

I have been requested to present myself before him, and we both know the court would find me guilty. It breaks me but I fear I must leave Kilkenny.

Wait for me, Roger. I am coming to you.

❧ February 1324 ❧

My knees sting. I crouch on the floor of Will's workroom. I ran from my inn when the word travelled to me. The Franciscan's paid men will come for me soon. Perhaps they have already armed their righteous bodies and left his door with the thrill of knowing they will be committing the Lord's sanctioned violence, forcing an old, but beautiful, woman into the prison.

Will lies on his settle, feet up, gazing at the ceiling, seemingly all fight gone from him, but I know he is merely gathering his rage, pulling it to him for the next fight, while I am on the floor, as if I am at a wake. Once my son was a jester, a laughing-eyed charmer, a little teasing prince. Now, like his mother, he is a vengeful sinner. How swiftly a child grows up. His hair is like a wolf's, grey and rough. His lips have thinned, as his father's did towards the end. He is what my first husband would have become had he lived longer.

"Get off the floor, Mother."

"No."

"Suit yourself."

Candles gutter. Yellow light leaps. I sit back on my feet and look up at his tapestry. Kilkenny is picked out in tiny stitches, the castle at one end, up on the hill at the other the cathedral and in between my inn. Smoke shoots up from my roof. Already I am burning.

"I have men."

"You can't kill the Franciscan."

He presses the heels of his hands to his eyes.

"If I have to," he says, "I'll buy a new roof for St. Canice's. I'm staying in Kilkenny."

"But I must go," I say.

He throws his hands aside and sits, finally facing me.

I push myself to stand, wrap my arms around my torso and cross the room to him. He jumps up, rubbing his face, shaking his head. The kiss he presses to my cheek is swift and cool. I lean my head on his shoulder, feel his body tense and relax. I don't tell him all will be well. I can't start lying to him in our last moments together.

🌿 A List of Those Arrested for Witchcraft 🌿

Robert of Bristol, John Galrussyn, Ellen Galrussyn, Syssok Galrussyn, William Payn de Boly, Alice, wife of Henry Faber, Eva de Brownestown, Annota Lange, Petronilla of Meath and her daughter, Sarah.

❧ February 1324 ❧

I am striding across the garden. The snow has melted, but the wind picks up the rain and hurls it at me. My cloak and the front of my tunic are drenched. An axe hangs from my hands. It is new, the handle freshly hewn, the weight in my hand well balanced. I swing my arms and bring it down. My mother's tree moans as metal tooth connects with bark. He took Petronilla. I would pray, pray, pray for her, but there's no use. I wish I could shroud what has been done, what will be done to her, with black blankets. I wish I could take away all the lanterns. Make it night. Extinguish the future, but my hands are powerless. As the bells of St. Mary's toll out, I slam the axe again and again until my mother's tree gives up and crashes into the river. Perhaps the tree will float away, but, no, escape is impossible now. I bend, grab the trunk and drag it away from the water's swift course.

A child's laugh disturbs me.

Basilia is sat on the frost-hardened ground. Her head is covered with an undyed sheep's-wool hood.

She pats her white cloak spread out on the ground.

Someone else will chop up my mother's tree for firewood. I lower myself down beside her, and the smell of cracked ice rises all around us. My hands are bleeding. She takes off her cap, revealing her soft, dark hair.

"Mama? Sarah?"

My tongue is too heavy. I cannot speak. There is no way to tell such a small child her mother and sister have been taken by Ledrede's men to the prison.

She holds out her hands, and there is a kitten, her amber head tilted slightly to one side, her black eyes knowing. Basilia places her cheek against the kitten.

I steady her elbows, and together we rise. She is beaming up at me and then down to the soft, little kitten in her hands. To and fro, her gaze goes, brimming with love. Now standing, she turns away from me towards the river, but she presses her back against my legs.

Already, I can see the tips of the sun's fingers on the sky. We must go.

"Basilia," I say, "have you ever wanted to see Dublin?"

She shakes her head.

"The cat will live here without you," I say.

She clutches the kitten to her chest. It wriggles, trying to break free from her tight grip. I take it from her hands, place it on the ground and carry the shrieking child through the side entrance and out to the street where a cart is waiting.

❧ All Souls' Day ❧

November 1324

Bells ring out a prayer to purify, with holy-agonising fire, all souls in purgatory. It's just after sunrise, and the sky is white above Kilkenny. The grey walls surrounding the bishop's garden are empty save for a flame-coloured cat, prowling. The ground is hard with frost. The fountain is frozen solid. The bells cease, and the door of Ossory's house springs open, but it is only a servant girl who tosses murky water onto the ground, blows on her red fingers and slams the door shut. Sacks have been tied around all the plants to protect them until the spring. They all were bred in the Mediterranean. They thrive in warm shade or a baking sky. Only an intractable mind would bring such plants to a windy, wet land, but just such a mind crafted this garden. All that remains within it of Ireland is the yew, standing at the edge, reaching for Kilkenny over the wall. The cat streaks along the wall and leaps into the tree. She nibbles on a poisonous berry. What will take a man's life sustains hers. She is gasping thirsty. She would drink blood if she could find it. She waits, but not for long. Again, the door swings open. Ledrede is shrunken in his brown and sombre cloak as if he were but a humble friar. This last year has taken the meat off him. Imprisonment in the castle under the orders of Roger Outlaw has left his face all grey valleys and white peaks. It has been tit for tat these months between the friends of Alice le Poer and the Bishop of Ossory, but on this day, he feels, finally he has won a small victory. He groans, stretches his arms over his head, cracking his elbows and wriggling his shoulders, a pleased expression on his lips. As the bells begin to clatter again, calling the masses of Kilkenny to prayer, he smiles up at the empty sky, clears his throat and hacks twice into his fist. He turns and puts his hand on the door as the bells cease again.

From the branch of the yew tree, the cat emits a desperate yowl, and Ledrede's shoulders leap up to his ears as if to stop the sound from entering him. Slowly, Ledrede turns and looks about the garden. There is a ridge between his wispy eyebrows. Leisurely, he cracks the knuckles one after the other, eyes casting about the garden, searching, until his gaze finds her, and he takes a tiny step back so small most would not notice it, but the cat has a keen sense of movement. She knows he's unsettled by her, but, all the same, he strides towards her, and instead of leaping onto the wall and running away, she stays on the branch. He is only one step away from the tree. She lets out a wild, angry sound. Emboldened, the bishop steps closer, reaches up towards her branch, mouth twitching into a smile, hands ready to grab. She puts her head to one side, as if to say, we both know how this day will end.

And then, because she cannot give him what he wants, she finally leaps onto the wall. She had planned to shadow him until the end, but she cannot bear it. She runs the length of the wall, jumps onto the sloping roof of a butcher's and climbs up towards the place where the smoke billows and the birds soar. She gains heights he could never reach. She turns once to look at him far below, watching her escape, a tiny little man swallowed by a city. She opens her mouth and howls into the dense air. He will have lost sight of her. He probably can't even hear her, but she doesn't need him to. She knows the image of her furred body is still blazing inside the dark rooms of his head. She leaves him behind and takes her habitual path over the roofs of the town, all slippery and stained with black mould. They are disintegrating, impermanent, damp, but if the winds change, any one might easily catch fire. Below her, flagging either side of the road, are grey, green and scarlet hats and so many white caps.

⌀

A roar rises up from the crowd near the castle, and the cat realises she cannot watch the woman burning. She leaps from house to house, shop to shop. Here it is oddly quiet. Few have remained in their homes. They have all gone to watch. They have gone to laugh, to weep. There is smoke in the air. It stings their eyes.

⌀

The sky is dimming. The cat walks on through the dark beside the black sheen of the River Nore. From a bridge, she leaps onto a barge, travelling all the way to the sea. In the morning, she will jump aboard a boat. She will take a covered cart through Wales without looking out to admire the mountains, and, many weeks later, she will stop in a walled garden, where she will tuck her head beneath her tail and rest a while, and later, after many seasons, she will open her eyes to summer and see the child Basilia playing with a ball beneath the nodding heads of the roses.

❧ England ❧

1331

A short man is gazing at the bare branches of an apple tree where a cat perches, seemingly asleep. The convent where the man finds himself is on the edge of a forest, clacking and clattering its icy branches, but behind the walls, the garden is quiet with frost and the still air is white with the light of late afternoon. The man shrinks into his heavy wool hood, his body stiff. Perhaps he senses he's being watched from the arcade which runs along two sides of the garden.

Beneath the shadows of the arcade, I, dressed in the vestments of a priest, watch him. I have been back and forth from the convent with Basilia for years now, befriending the abbess, making this our occasional retreat from business. Today, I brought the priest's clothes with me and waited until all the nuns were at their prayers before dressing myself as a holy man, baring my grey hair, so I could meet their visitor. Since I left Ireland, I have worn a man's name and clothes, and in the small town nearby, I own a seaside inn where I trade wool and coins and gossip. Madness trails through letters from Will and Roger: Arnold le Poer, my late husband's cousin, has died in prison for his stand against the Franciscan in my stead; Ellen and Syssok Galrussyn and Alice Faber were all burned (Sarah too, and still a child); Ledrede was blissfully humiliated—called to the court to justify his deranged actions—but he copied me and fled, and I knew soon he would pass through England on his way to plead his case in Avignon, stopping in monasteries and convents on the way. This convent stands on the coast looking out to France, directly in the path for all those fleeing.

I watch him now beneath the apple tree, the man who was once Bishop of Ossory, and I am disappointed. I expected him to be ranging to and fro, his lines flowing with menace, but what I see is the same small and seemingly innocuous man, his hands bare, fingers blunt and white.

On quiet feet I approach him, grasp his shoulder, and to my pleasure he startles at my touch.

"You seem anguished."

I offer a gentle, distant smile, one any convent's priest might give to a lonely traveller.

"Oh, no, no," he says, his voice more frantic and high-pitched than I remember. "Thank you, Brother."

He smiles at me, places a hand in thanks on my arm—I am one of his kind after all—and turns back to look up into the branches of the apple tree. The cat yawns, stretches and leaps onto the wall.

"Does the apple tree make you think of the Fall?" I ask.

He gazes at the cat prancing back and forth, her hips swaying. He seems mesmerised.

"Are you unwell?" I say.

He shakes his head.

"I was only thinking," he says, eyes still fastened to the cat, "how much this garden reminds me of one I used to know."

His eyes are shot through with red. Perhaps, like me, he has slept ill these past seven years.

"Where was this other garden?" I say.

"Kilkenny," he says.

"A famous place of late. You must tell me all about it. Come. Join me by the kitchen fire for a warm drink. It is quiet as the nuns are fasting and deep in prayer all evening." I glance up and down his gaunt frame. "I am sure we will find some other sustenance for you there too."

The sky has turned orange as if the light is bursting up for one last explosive breath before the darkness takes it. He looks once more at the tree. There's one reddish apple, shrivelled but still clinging to the branch. The cat leaps, lands on the ground and streaks for the convent in search of mice.

"You have an infestation here?" he asks.

"Oh, just one or two creatures visiting."

$\mathscr{D}$

I direct Ledrede to the kitchen, and alone I pass down the corridor and open a door. Basilia lies in her bed, chest rising and falling. All I have, not that it's much, is left to her. She may remain here with the nuns, continue running the inn or perhaps she will travel to new places, tasting strange fruit and sleeping beneath purple skies. I pause to watch her, to see life go on and on inside her. I long to fall to my knees, lay my head by hers and stay until she wakes. Together we would return to our inn and pretend, as we have done these seven years, that I am her parent, that I am faultless, but she will be a woman in a few years and come to know all. Lips belonging to people I don't know will tell her mine was the hand that led her mother and sister to the fire, and on hearing this she will give me no mercy. She is fierce like her mother and a dreamer like her father. She will abandon me. I can't wait for her to act first. Instead, I leave without touching her. I shut the door, bolt her in. I know her. I have raised her to hate the Franciscan. If she discovers he is sleeping here, she will slice open his throat while he dreams, and even I can't conceal his blood from a court. She is a dark-skinned girl. For her there would be no mercy. We could run to France, flee beyond to Italy, but we would always be running. She would never be free. I will save her from herself, and, come sunrise, the nuns will release her.

*

The kitchen is too warm after the garden's bite. Already, my hair is sticking to my neck, and my vestments are saturated with my sweat. Flour has been left spilt on the large table, seed scattered on the floor. By the hearth, the cat rolls in ash.

Ledrede wipes his greasy mouth with a kerchief and throws a chicken bone into the fire.

"You may have heard of my work," he says.

"I know who you are," I say. "Your name is almost as notorious as Alice Kyteler's." I lift my hair where it is stuck to my neck. "But your deeds were divinely influenced and hers, well . . . you saw something in her, a malicious fire perhaps, or an uncanny, free-thinking brazenness."

He coughs, takes a chicken wing from the plate and, eyeing the cat who has curled up between his feet, he takes a bite.

"If you have not already," I say, "don't mention your name to my nuns. It would overexcite them."

"I too have an abhorrence of high-spirited women," he says, his mouth full of half-chewed white flesh. "But meeting churchmen such as yourself makes me feel my work has not gone unappreciated, despite what some have led me to feel."

"Well, yes. Well." I force a smile, shake my head and the smile falls away. I look up and force another smile. "I have thought long about this case. What has bothered me for so many years is why."

"Why?"

"What was her reason for killing her husbands?"

"The Devil's word—and avarice. She would have done anything for money."

"No."

"Excuse me?"

"There is no thinking man or woman's answer. She just did it. She just killed. It was baser, all of it, like those two in the garden before they fell. There just is what was done, and the sadness and guilt, not from what men like you preach, but in the self, in knowing those men were all children once, gazing up at a tree or the stars and feeling the expansiveness of the world and themselves within it. That's all the knowing there is."

"You think her an animal, but I met her. She was entirely a woman. Cunning, vicious, deceptive."

"You say you knew her, so I must believe you."

Ledrede rubs his left eyelid with a fingertip. "I see eccentricity breeds in these forgotten nunneries."

He believes me to be some outlandish priest, left to fester too long with women. If only he knew.

"Here," I say, "all are free to indulge in their true selves."

"That is a dangerous approach in a nest of women."

"I doubt they will harm you." I cough into my fist, and when I take it away, my palm is dotted with blood. Since leaving Kilkenny, I have been dogged by this sickness, the coughing, the weakness, the aching and, lastly, the blood that signals the slow end of me.

Ledrede picks crumbs off his lap, dabbing them onto his tongue. Pleasantly, silence stretches between us. I put a small pot of broth over the embers. The fire hisses and cracks. Soon we will be gone from this place. Soon some other woman will stir the flames.

Wind drives down the chimney shaft and blows smoke into the kitchen. Ledrede covers his mouth and nose with his sleeve. I hand him a steaming cup of broth, which he takes with murmured thanks.

"You must be bored of talking about the case," I say. Tears from the smoke burn my cheeks.

"It has been the work of my life." Ledrede smiles at the fire, eyes bloodshot and watering. "Few understand the magnitude of the problem, too distracted by coins and flesh."

"What did she look like?" The light from the fire is blunt like an old knife, and in it he looks brutal yet more shrunken than ever before. He is just a small man, but he killed her. He killed all of them.

"She looked old," he says, blinking rapidly, "but wanton."

His lips part as if he were still hungry. He glances away from me to stare again at the flames and tweaks a piece of chicken from his teeth. He hasn't touched his broth.

"So evil looks like a wanton woman," I say. "It is so simple. I wonder I never thought of this myself."

"You are too led by your nuns." He flicks another piece of meat from his mouth.

"And Petronilla?"

"She oiled Kyteler's stick and rode it herself. She pleasured herself while watching her mistress fornicate with demons, but you know all this. You followed the case."

"Petronilla's word wasn't sound, yet the case was built on it."

"I was there in God's guise. I could judge her answers."

"Wouldn't you admit to heresy if you were being tortured?"

He shakes his head, staring at me now with a kind of fascination.

"And," I say, because I cannot seem to stop, "wasn't it well-known that Petronilla had been eating bread made from spoiled grain? The grain that turns you demented with nightmarish imagery."

Slowly, Ledrede stands. All the colour has drained from his face.

"Do you think she lives?" I say.

I find I am standing too. Seven years I have been waiting for him.

"What manner of man are you?" His broth tumbles from his hand to the floor. It spreads wide. He's backing away from me towards the door. His lumpen little face is ashen. He shakes his head, looking at his feet, and I am just one small step away from him, the cat now circling my legs.

Finally, he looks at me.

"You are from Kilkenny," he says, fumbling with the door. He opens it and stares hard at me, then shakes his head and steps daintily into the passage.

He came in search of me, just like all the others, all the men I refused, all the men I married. These last years I have been hidden, waiting for him. But I had no plan to torture him the way he tortured her, nor end him in a fire the way, alive, he burned her. I have never thought blow by blow how to act, and now, although I want to see him suffer, I don't want to be the one to end him.

"I watched her burning," he says. "It is beautiful, so inspiring to see God's work. She screamed her mistress's name."

His hands are delicately folded in front of him.

"You lie," I say. "It was her daughters' names. Sarah. Basilia."

My face aches, as if I have sat too close to the flames.

If he were dead, his stare would look dull, his smile uncanny, but with eyes shining, he smiles the smile of a man who was in on the pretence from the beginning. He smiles as if he's known me all along.

"Little Franciscan," I say, "you will leave now. A place full of free young women—imagine what they might do to you."

❧ The Trees ❧

I leave the convent by the side entrance, lighting my way through the end of the night with a lamp. It dimly illuminates the puckered frozen ground just beyond my feet. Ahead, I sense the height of the forest reaching skywards. Ice cracks and shatters in the trees, and in the violet dark I am held.

I place the lantern on the ground and shed my clothes, remove my priest's hood, the leather belt, the alb and my shoes. I am old, and I am naked, opening my arms wide to the wind's bite. Once I was hit by lightning and caught fire. My skin still wears the white scars like branches. I am a rare case. Once brightly I burned, I drew them all to me and consumed them all, unwittingly and wittingly, in my fire.

Now, I breathe out, finally cold. For the first time in my life, there's nowhere I need to hurry back to. I don't look back. I step between the trees, open my mouth and roar.

A Note on the Writing

"the love-lorn Lady Kyteler"
W. B. Yeats, *Nineteen Hundred and Nineteen* (1921)

Judy Chicago's installation *The Dinner Party*
(1974–79) displays a place at the table for Petronilla
de Meath. The plate holds images of a book,
a candle, a bell and a cauldron.
All are encapsulated in fire.

This book is a work of fiction, but it was inspired by a woman who lived.

It is worth noting that, in Medieval Ireland, the official New Year was marked on 25 March, Lady Day, which was the date when the angel supposedly announced to Mary that she was pregnant with the baby Jesus. However, for the purpose of this novel, I have marked the dates by our modern tradition, the New Year falling on 1 January.

I am particularly grateful to the work of Finbar Dwyer and his book *Life in Medieval Ireland: Witches, Spies and Stockholm Syndrome*. It is now worn from many reads. Katherine Harvey's *The Fires of Lust: Sex in the Middle Ages* gave a fascinating insight into attitudes to sex during Alice's lifetime.

The scholarship of Anne Neary was invaluable to the writing of this book, particularly her scholarship on the trial.

The work of St. John Drelincourt Seymour gave a key but deeply distressing account of *A contemporary narrative of the proceedings against Dame Alice Kyteler*, which was written in Latin by Ledrede or someone under his instruction. His account has already been written so I only allowed Ledrede to intrude onto the pages when I felt it absolutely necessary.

I am also deeply grateful to Kilkenny Archaeological Society for allowing me to access their archives, and to the wonderful volunteer librarians there who tirelessly went back and forth from the shelves and allowed me to photograph all the texts so that I could consult them during late-night writing sessions.

I deliberately chose not to illustrate what should never have been done to Petronilla. I did not wish to add to her trauma, nor the readers', by reanimating it.

Alice Kyteler is firmly imprinted on the pages of Irish history, but if it weren't for the case of witchcraft brought against her, we probably never would have known she lived. Yet, like many women, her perspective has been lost. This novel is an attempt to give her a voice again.

I am grateful to all the people who in ways, little and great, assisted me in bringing this book to the page. My thanks to: Orion, my star, my baby. I began this novel while you were growing inside me, and now both of you are released into the world. Love you, little one.

Art, an encouraging voice and always the laughter in the hard times.

My family. First, my mother, Maureen, for her fierce and constant faith that I could do it, even sleep-deprived. To my father, James, for his passion for history which he instilled in me young. To my sisters, Rosie, Joanna and Alexa, for your laughter and kindness from afar. To the Scots, Irish and Brazilians, thank you for all your support and love.

My dear writing friends: my Bath Spa gang (Clare, Susie and Chrissy) who cheered me on from afar; Yasmina Floyer for your voice recordings—I mean podcasts—that nurtured me through all the ups and downs of writing Alice, I honestly couldn't have done it without you; Jenny Mustard for suffering the early drafts and giving me such insightful notes that meant I had no choice but to make this book better. But David Mustard, you are still my favourite honorary woman, and the best host for bonkers writers I will ever meet.

The many editors whose talented hands have touched this book: Jo Dingley, who told me it was a good idea and encouraged me to begin; Aa'Ishah Hawton, who kindly helped to nurture the first draft into something that was book-shaped; Diana Miller, whose generous and always brilliant insight made me see the novel with new eyes; and finally Leah Woodburn, who with grace and brilliance brought Alice to completion.

Everyone at Canongate and Knopf—I am blessed to have your force and brilliance behind my words.

The champion and talent who is my agent, Hellie Ogden. Thank you for your beautiful edits and friendship. My thanks also to Hellie's right-hand woman, Ma'suma Amiri, for putting up with my short stories and for all your kind emails.

The lifeline that was Sheffield Writers' Development Grant which I was able to use to hire childcare and grab hours at a time with Alice. My gratitude in particular to Maria de Souza and Stefan Tobler.

My two new heroes, my PhD supervisors at Sheffield Hallam University, Professor Harriet Tarlo and Dr. Alison Twells, who are supporting me with my next wild adventure into novel writing, and are just generally rocks that I now can't do without.

Last, but obviously not least, Alice. I am beyond grateful to you for allowing me to inhabit your history and give you a voice. Thank you.

A NOTE ABOUT THE AUTHOR

Molly Aitken grew up on the south coast of Ireland. Her first novel, *The Island Child*, was longlisted for the Authors' Club First Novel Award. Her short fiction has appeared in *Ploughshares*, for which she won the Alice Hoffman Prize for Fiction, and has been dramatized for BBC Radio 4. She is currently studying for a PhD in Creative Writing and History at Sheffield Hallam University.